CONSUMED BY FIRE

BLOOD & MAGIC: FIREBORN - FIVE

DANIELLE ANNETT

coffee and
CHARACTERS

l

Also by Danielle Annett

Blood & Magic: Fireborn

Praise for the Blood & Magic series

Cursed by Fire

"Oh my GOODNESS! I completely devoured this book in one sitting it was THAT GOOD!"
—*Cocktails and Books Blog*

"I thought Cursed by Fire was an awesome read and a great introduction to the series. I can't fault it in any way and thoroughly enjoyed it and am looking forward to more."
—*Book Passion for Life*

"I personally am a Kate Daniels fan, and I loved this series."
—*Amazon Reviewer*

Kissed by Fire

"I love how Danielle Annett writes. Her books are so intriguing, action packed, and unique."

"Danielle Annett's BRANDED BY FIRE is scorching hot."
—*Amazon Reviewer*

"Branded by Fire is the best one yet (and the other 3 books in the series rock!)"
—*Sapphyria's Book Blog*

Consumed by Fire

"Aria is badass"
—*Amazon Reviewer*

"Another fast paced installment of the Blood & Magic series. Aria's sass and badassery keeps me coming back for more."
—*Amazon Reviewer*

"When an author can leave you hanging and wanting more; then that is a brilliant author."
—*The Avid Reader*

Forged by Fire

"Love it. Worth the wait"
—*Amazon Reviewer*

"The conclusion to this series was everything I expected and more. Besides thinking as aria as my bff and watching her grow thru the series I've also watched this author grow. I look forward to reading her next series! She surprised me in this last book and I'm so crazy that I rarely get surprised! "
—*Amazon Reviewer*

Chapter One

I hated people sometimes. I especially hated people who tried to kill me. And the number of people who tried to kill me grew higher with each passing day.

How the hell I wound up babysitting the woman who *only seven days* ago had tried to kill me was a mystery.

Why would anyone in their right mind agree to that?

Clearly I wasn't in my right mind. Because here I was, sitting in a leather recliner, and staring at her comatose body as she lay in a bed inside the Pacific Northwest Compound. The same Pack Compound where I lived.

The Compound was seventy-four thousand square feet nestled on one hundred and seven acres. She could be on one end and I on the other and it still wouldn't be enough space between us.

I ground my teeth together. I should be the one relaxing in bed, but no. Instead I was babysitting Dia Ryholt.

My skin vibrated with energy.

She'd given me a concussion, two bruised ribs, a sprained wrist, and a hell of a lot of scrapes, gashes, and bruises. As a psyker—someone with psychokinetic abilities—I healed faster than your average human, but nowhere near as fast as a shifter. My bones still ached and now and then my wrist would twinge.

Having her here made my blood boil. This was my home. Sure I'd only recently moved in, but that was beside the point. I belonged here.

She didn't.

The temperature in the room ratcheted up several degrees.

Shit.

I folded one leg over the other and closed my eyes.

Breathe. That's it. Relax.

I popped my neck and rolled my shoulders back. The room was silent save for the tapping of my leather boot on the hard stone floor and the steady inhale and exhale of my breaths.

She's in a coma. She can't hurt you, I reminded myself.

Not that it helped.

I lifted one eyelid to make sure Dia was still there.

You could never be too sure with telekinetics. One second they were there, and the next... Well, you got the idea.

But she was still there. Right where she'd been the last seven days and seven nights. And at the rate we were going, she was right where she'd be for the next week or more.

I scrubbed my hands over my face and glared daggers at her.

Dia's jet- black hair stretched over a pale, lavender pillow and a small smile curved up the corners of her lips. Freckles dusted her high cheekbones and her chest expanded with each inhale of breath. Closed lids hid what I knew to be blue-gray eyes so clear it was like looking into a bottomless ocean.

She had the same eyes as her brother. The same jet-black hair. But where Inarus' skin was bronzed like desert sand, Dia's was alabaster white.

If it weren't for the IV in her right forearm and the feeding tube in her nose, you'd think she was sleeping.

She looked peaceful. Well rested, even.

It made me want to punch her in her too-pretty face. *Hard.*

I seriously thought about doing it, too. A quick glance at the door assured me that the coast was clear. Declan had gone to a meeting with the witches a little over an hour ago, and Inarus was back at Sanborn Place coordinating repairs. Neither should be back for at least another ten to fifteen minutes or more.

I chewed on my lower lip. The Human Alliance Corporation had trashed my office in an attempt to track me down. And the dark-haired beauty in front of me was one of theirs. A telekinetic in her prime and unfortunately related to Inarus Ryholt.

Inarus was my lone employee at Sanborn Place and a friend.

It felt weird calling him that, when not so long ago he'd been my enemy. But things had changed. Inarus had proven more than once that he could be trusted.

He'd be really pissed if I hit her.

So here I was trusting that in time he would sort things out where his sister was concerned. He'd asked that the Pack spare her, and as a favor to me, Declan had.

A part of me wished I'd never asked Declan to hold back. But Inarus had saved my ass more times than I could count. Even when we weren't fighting on the same side. The least I could do was watch over his sister and refrain from killing her. I owed him that much.

But, dammit, I really wanted to hit her.

I rocked back and forth in my chair and cursed. "You're better than that," I told myself.

I wasn't. Not really. But we all lied to ourselves from time to time.

Telling myself that hitting a woman in a coma was beneath me was better than admitting that the only reason I hadn't already punched her in her stupid face was because it would leave a mark.

And you could guess how that would go over.

Maybe I could just light her hair on fire. A small flicker of a flame.

I smiled.

Fire would be fun. I could just singe eight or nine inches off. She was probably vain. I wondered how she'd feel to wake up with those pretty locks gone.

My smiled faded. How would I explain *that* to Inarus?

"Err … I'm sorry. I lost control of my pyrokinetic abilities but on the upside, I managed to only burn off her hair."

I snorted. Yeah, that would go over well.

I resigned myself to sitting and staring. Because if looks could kill, she'd already be dead ten times over.

Someone cleared their throat, and I jerked my head up to find Declan Valkenaar—Alpha to the Pacific Northwest Pack and my mate—standing in the doorway.

My heart rate picked up as our eyes collided. Gold flecks filled his emerald gaze, and a light dusting of white-blonde hair shadowed his hard, square jaw.

Heat pooled in my stomach, and I sucked in a breath.

Declan stalked into the room. It was the only way I could describe it. He moved on silent feet with long, graceful strides like the predator he was. His muscles bunched with each movement, hinting at the coiled strength hidden beneath the thin fabric of his clothes.

"Don't sneak up on me like that," I chided to cover my reaction to his proximity. Butterflies decided to do cartwheels in my stomach. And I gripped the armrest of my seat to keep from reaching out for him.

He laughed and smiled a wicked smile. "Talking to yourself again, Aria?"

I rolled my eyes. "No. Just rationalizing." I stood from the chair and, without conscious thought, moved closer to where he stood. I caught myself, but it was already too late.

Declan rested his palm on my lower back and captured my gaze with his again. "How's that working out for you?"

Dressed in dark denim jeans, work boots, and a forest-green

thermal shirt, Declan looked like your average well-muscled male.

Until you caught the shifter glint in his eyes and recognized the ropes of corded muscle that bunched beneath his shirt.

Declan would never be average. He was a Siberian weretiger. And he was Alpha. Dominance radiated from his skin. At the ripe age of twenty-four, he'd seized control of the Pack, and nine years later, he still held it with an iron grip.

He turned his Alpha stare on me.

If I were a weaker person, I would turn my gaze to the floor; slurring my words and praying for him to hurry up and leave before I peed myself.

Lucky for me, I wasn't weak.

But I was a woman, and I wasn't blind. Butterflies continued to dance in my stomach, and my body swayed in his direction for just a second before I jerked myself back. "Fucking peachy. Why don't you turn off your headlights and give me an update?"

Declan laughed, a rich sound that vibrated deep in his chest. He turned toward me and placed both hands on my hips. "Does it always have to be business?" he asked, a wicked glint in his eyes.

I shrugged my shoulders in a noncommittal gesture. Of course it didn't have to be all business. Lord knew that my lady bits certainly didn't want it to be, but I didn't need him knowing that. It would go straight to his head, and he was arrogant enough as it was.

Declan's gaze captivated my full attention. A small furrow formed between his brows when he didn't get the welcome he'd been expecting. "The witches have an idea. We should have answers soon."

"Good. Maybe then we'll be able to get on with our lives."

He nodded, pulling me into an embrace.

I melted against his chest with a sigh of relief.

"We have a plan. But that doesn't mean we have to wait to explore our lives together."

"Mmmm …" I closed my eyes and breathed in the scent of pine and mint that was uniquely Declan. "Is now really the best time to—"

Declan cut me off, taking me by surprise with the firm press of his lips against mine.

Before I could react, he drew back and tucked my head against his chest.

"We don't have to figure everything out right now. She isn't going anywhere. It can all wait while we work on us."

If only that were true. With the HAC still determined to eliminate paranormals, we needed answers, and Dia was the only one who could give them to us. We'd have interrogated her already if it weren't for the fact that she was a telekinetic with the added ability to teleport. If we woke her up, she'd teleport herself out of the Compound without bothering to see what it was we were after.

Hence Declan and his visit to the witches. We were hoping they'd have a spell that could bind her abilities so she couldn't teleport herself to freedom.

And with the newly formed alliance between the Pacific Northwest Pack and the Evergreen witches, there was a good chance they'd even be willing to share it.

"I know we have a lot to sort out, but I can't focus on a future if the threat of my mother and the HAC looms over it.

We stood there for several seconds, and Declan drew small circles on my lower back with one hand while the other gripped me against his muscled body.

I listened to the steady beat of his heart, taking comfort in his strength.

"No more waiting. I can't take it anymore." I was sick and tired of looking over my shoulder. The Human Alliance Corporation—or HAC—needed to be stopped.

"She's your mother. Are you sure—"

Fury consumed me so quickly that fire broke out across my skin.

I spun on my heel and paced to the opposite side of the room. "She's not my mother. My mother died seven years ago along with my father. That woman isn't my mother." I folded my arms over my chest.

Sure, I was probably overreacting, but you would too if you'd been through what I had.

The ground shook.

"Aria—"

"I know!" I snapped.

I took a deep breath and closed my eyes. *Get it together.* A storm of psychokinetic power thrummed through my veins.

"What did the witches say?" I needed the subject change to get my mind off my mother, and the realization that the woman I'd grown up loving was a monster who'd instigated her husband's murder and abandoned her only child because she saw me as an abomination.

The air stirred around me.

Declan sighed but continued without acknowledging my slip in control. "Olivia said there's a spell they can do to bind Dia's abilities. It will be a day or two before they can forge the spell into a wrist cuff, but when they're finished, we should be able to wake her without risk of her teleporting.

I nodded. "Good. It's about time we got some answers. I'm sick of being on the defensive."

Declan strode toward me. He cupped the side of my face and stroked his thumb along my cheek. "You're not fighting this— fighting her—alone. I have you. Always."

I leaned into his touch. I knew he had my back. But it was nice hearing the words out loud anyway.

Declan was my mate. He would always be there to fight my battles with me. But I was still getting used to being able to depend on someone else—and having that person depend on me in turn.

"Thank you." I reached up and kissed him. Just a light press of my lips on his.

I wasn't ready to jump him even if my lady bits wanted me to. Our relationship was still new. But satisfaction thrummed through me when his eyes widened and his heart rate quickened beneath the press of my palm.

A beaming smile spread out over his face. He leaned down, and I angled my face upward to reach him ...

And then my phone rang.

Declan growled and pulled away from me. "Every time—"

I turned away to hide my smile and pulled my phone from my pocket. "Naveed."

"You might want to get down here," Inarus said.

Every one of my nerve endings went on high alert. "Did something happen? Was there an attack? Dammit, I knew—"

"No. None of that. Calm down."

I paced back and forth across the room. "Well, then what is it?" Agitation coursed through me.

Inarus sighed. "There have been some bumps with repairs."

"What kind of bumps?" How hard was it to replace floors and slap on a fresh coat of paint? Sure, the door and a few windows needed to be repaired too, but it was all pretty straight forward.

"It's hard to explain. Do you have time to come by Sanborn Place today?"

I eyed Dia's comatose body. She wasn't going anywhere.

"Yeah, I'll be right there."

Warm breath caressed my shoulder, and Declan pressed his body against mine as I snapped my phone closed.

"I'm coming with you." Declan nuzzled my shoulder.

"I figured you'd say that." I leaned back into him.

"Who was on the phone?"

I rolled my eyes. "As if you couldn't hear."

A growl vibrated in his chest.

"You're going to have to play nice eventually," I told him.

Inarus and Declan weren't each other's biggest fans. It might have something to do with Inarus betraying me, playing a role in a shifter's death, and then putting the moves on me when Declan considered me his. But that was all water under the bridge now.

If I could move past it, so could they.

Declan only glowered.

Sometimes he was too stubborn for his own good.

Chapter Two

It took us forty minutes to get from the secluded Pack Compound and into downtown Spokane where Sanborn Place was located.

I rode passenger as Declan drove the Pack's burnt orange Hummer down the freeway before taking the Lincoln street exit.

"You'll have to driv—"

I lifted a hand to stop him. "No. I'm not driving this tank on wheels. I have a car. I don't need to drive yours." I shivered in my seat. "Besides, it wouldn't feel right." Driving this monstrosity of a vehicle would be a slap in the face to my baby.

Declan's hands tightened on the steering wheel. "You're being unreasonable. You need a car. I'm providing you one."

"I have a car. My Civic is in the shop. I'll have it back in a week. Two, tops. I'll be fine until then."

Inarus had agreed to port me around if I needed to go anywhere, anyway. Given that worked, our destinations usually coincided with one another.

I hated teleporting. It made my skin itch and my insides feel like they were riding a roller coaster from hell, but it definitely cut down on the commute.

Declan growled beside me. He'd been there when Inarus had made the offer. And a small piece of me had gloated when he'd snarled at the suggestion then, too.

"Your Civic is dead. It's not coming back. It's gone to junkyard heaven and you need to come to grips. Just drive this car on the way home. You'll like it."

"No." I didn't want to replace my Civic. The mechanic said there was hope. And I was choosing to hold on to it.

Declan made an exasperated noise.

That made two of us.

I didn't want this orange tank. I wanted *my car*. My 2010 two-door Honda Civic that I'd had decked out to take on a tank much like this one.

It'd sported quarter inch bulletproof glass, a reinforced frame, and was encased in high mobility armor all the way down to the undercarriage.

It'd been virtually indestructible.

At least until Aiden—one of my mother's telekinetic henchmen—had used a grinder to cut me out of it after ramming into my car with his truck at high speed on a deserted street.

Now my poor little Civic sat outside the Compound looking like a dilapidated husk of its former self.

But Aiden was dead.

I smiled.

He'd deserved it.

Of course, he'd died only after he'd tried—and failed—to abduct me. Then succeeded in hiring someone else to abduct me, strapped me down to a cold metal table, and tried to suck my pyrokinetic abilities out of me.

But the joke was on him.

Because, instead, I managed to suck *his* telekinetic abilities out of *him* and, as I'd expected, pyskers couldn't survive without their psyker bits and pieces. Psychokinesis was the core of who and what we were. Try to separate it from our human skins and well… it didn't work out.

"What if—"

"Nope." I drummed my fingers along the door with a grin. There wasn't anything Declan could say to convince me to give up on my car.

And there was that growl again.

I could see the tension in the hard line of his jaw but didn't bother addressing it. Declan was dominant and protective. He was also possessive and a control freak.

The car might not seem like a big thing, but it was. If I gave him an inch, he'd take a mile.

He wouldn't mean to. Taking over was a just part of who he was. It was a part of being Alpha. But it was a part of him that would smother me if I let it. He had to fight the need to dominate and protect me, and he usually managed. But I had to manage expectations in this relationship.

I needed my independence like I needed air to breathe.

I didn't want to look back one day and realize I was an Alpha's mate and *only an Alpha's mate.*

Most women—especially post Awakening—would welcome his protection with open arms.

However, I wasn't most women.

We pulled into the parking garage and Declan turned off the ignition and released the steering wheel, but made no move to get out of the car.

I waited. Whatever he had to say needed to be said, or he'd be insufferable the rest of the day.

I saw a flash of gold in his eyes through my peripheral.

I waited some more.

The gold ebbed, and he shook himself.

"I don't like him…"

Here we go.

"…putting his hands on my mate."

Here's what it boiled down to. Jealousy.

"It's not intimate. He grabs my hand or touches my shoulder, and away we go."

He was making a bigger deal out of this than it needed to be.

Declan's upper lip curled, exposing his canines that thankfully hadn't elongated. Yet.

"I don't give a shit if it's intimate. No man, human, shifter, or otherwise, should have his hands on my mate."

I got that. I did.

If I saw a woman touch Declan, it would make my blood boil, too. But I knew the difference between an intimate touch and a casual one.

"I don't want your car—"

He snarled, and gold flecks filled his irises once more.

I shoved down the immature teenager inside of me that wanted to tell him to fuck off. I wouldn't let him control my life. But I knew this was hard for him, and if I could make it easier in some small way without giving in entirely, I would.

"But I'll use the company car until mine is fixed."

"You will?" Relief washed over his face.

I fought the urge to roll my eyes, knowing that in a few moments Declan would change his mind.

I shrugged my shoulders. "Yeah. It'll take me longer to get back home each day, and it increases the risk of my mother's men tracking me, but it's not a big deal. I don't mind the commute, and I can take what she has to throw at me."

Declan's brows furrowed.

Okay, maybe I hadn't shoved the immature part of me down far enough, because now he was trying to figure out what was more important.

My safety. Or his jealousy of Inarus.

Safety won out.

"Just port with the damned psyker," he growled.

He opened the driver side door and stepped out.

I hid my smile with the back of my hand.

"You sure?" I followed him to the staircase that would take us to street level and the doors of Sanborn Place. "Because I want you to be comfortable. If Inarus—"

"I'm sure."

With a wide grin, I slipped my hand into his and walked upstairs.

His grip tightened on mine for just a moment.

I squeezed back and flicked my eyes toward him.

Heat filled his gaze, and I suddenly had the urge to stop right there on that flight of stairs and haul him down to me. I didn't. But that didn't change the fact that I really wanted to.

"Your emotions are leaking," I told him and hoped he'd get a lid on it.

The mate bond made two people closer than I'd ever thought possible. It allowed us to experience emotions from one another. And right now I felt lots of hot and sexy things that made my toes curl and a flush rush up my neck.

"We have rules," I reminded him and ignored the need to fan myself.

As a condition to giving this whole mating thing a go, I'd enacted a six-month no-sex rule. But I was seriously reconsidering that decision.

Visions of our legs intertwined and skin on skin assailed me.

With shifter strength and speed, Declan lifted me off the ground and had my legs wrapped around his waist and my back pressed firmly against the stairwell wall.

He nuzzled my neck and goosebumps broke out over my skin.

God that felt good. So good.

"You said no sex. That doesn't mean we can't—"

I gasped and braced my hands on his shoulders, but I didn't know if I meant to push him away or pull him closer.

"Yes. Yes it does." My voice was breathless. "Because not sex with you will lead to sex with you. Put me down." My heart hammered in my chest, and it took every ounce of my willpower not to melt into his embrace.

Declan chuckled, and his heat-filled gaze held mine. "You sure?"

No. I definitely was not sure. In fact, I was pretty sure I wanted anything but for him to let me go.

But I didn't voice that aloud.

Instead, I swallowed hard and nodded.

With deliberate slowness, he set me down on my feet.

I straightened my shirt and readjusted the twin daggers I had sheathed at my waist. Releasing a deep breath, I tried to slow my racing heart.

Declan looked cool as a cucumber. His Alpha mask back in place and his expression relaxed.

Not fair.

We climbed the remaining steps to the office, and he opened the door.

"After you." Declan's grin was filled with mischief, and I couldn't figure out why until I came face to face with three shifters with smug expressions on their faces and a very confused Inarus.

My cheeks burned. Damned shifter hearing.

I turned and smacked Declan on the arm. "Not cool."

Declan cupped my ass and leaned down to whisper in my ear, "Just claiming what is already mine."

Chapter Three

D iamond Rock Construction was on site helping Inarus get everything back in order. Between their manpower and his TK abilities, it looked like they were almost done.

Thank God.

The front window and doors had already been replaced. Carpet had been stripped out. And most of the furniture that needed to be removed was set-aside in a pile, leaving the office open and ready for us to bring in new furniture.

"You guys are ahead of schedule." I scanned the room taking in the new hardwood floors—that I couldn't afford—and the freshly painted walls that were now a soft seafoam green instead of their original gray.

"You made upgrades." It wasn't a question.

But Christian Kennedy—the Diamond Rock Construction contractor—answered it anyway "Just a few at Declan's request. Hardwood floors, new paint, new fixtures on all the doors, and—"

I held up a hand, halting him, and turned to Declan. "Sanborn Place can't afford this."

"They don't have to. I've taken care of—"

"No." My blood heated. Dammit. I couldn't believe he did this.

Turning to Inarus, I forced my voice to remain even. "Care to explain? I thought I made myself pretty clear on what was supposed to happen here."

He sighed and sent a scathing glare toward Declan. "I know. That's why I called. These are his men. Whose orders do you think they follow?"

I put my hands on my hips. "You and I," I told Declan. "Will discuss this later. And you—" I met Christian's gaze and held it.

Silver flooded his chocolate colored eyes, his beast rising to the challenge.

"You are not authorized to do any more upgrades at *my* place of business. Are we clear?"

The tension in the room thickened, but I refused to look away. Shifters took direct eye contact as a challenge. Usually I avoided it, if only to prevent their panties from getting in a bunch. I wasn't a shifter, and I didn't follow their customs. But Christian needed to know that I was in charge here.

A growl sounded behind me. *Declan.* But I still didn't turn.

Christian's eyes flicked toward Declan and back again, so fast I almost missed the movement.

Three more seconds passed. His lips curled back exposing a hint of fang.

Bad move, buddy.

My heart rate quickened, and I reached for my daggers. I didn't want this to get physical, but if that was what his beast needed …

A roar exploded out of Declan that had every one of my hairs standing on end.

Christian took two steps back.

"Are you challenging my mate?"

See? Bad move.

Christian paled. "I … I would never …"

As funny as it was, I didn't want to get a reputation of Declan having to fight all my battles. "Stop it." I turned toward Declan, taking in the fury in his eyes and the lines of tension in his face. "I'm not a shifter. It's not a challenge just because—"

He narrowed his gold-flecked gaze on me, and I met it.

"See? Not a challenge." I smiled.

Declan made an exasperated noise. "This isn't a joke. I can't allow—"

"It's nothing. And Christian isn't going to perform any more upgrades, right?" I raised my brows, and he nodded.

"No ma'am. No more upgrades."

"Good. Now that we've got that out of the way, you can show me what you've done and what you have left to do. I want copies of all the receipts. Sanborn Place will pay for all of it."

Declan tried to speak, but I held my hand up. "No. I won't take your charity. This is my business. Mine. It is separate from the Pack, and I am wholly responsible for it. If you want to help me, don't approve upgrades I can't afford. I won't accept charity, even from you."

Declan's lip curled, but he nodded. Twenty minutes later we'd covered the remaining work list, crossed a few things off of it to save my budget, and made a plan to reopen our doors early next week.

With any luck, business would pick up and things would go back to normal.

Christian and Declan were on the other side of the office discussing something I couldn't hear when Inarus approached me.

"I'm sorry. I would have called sooner but …"

"It's fine."

Inarus stared down at me, his blue-gray eyes piercing. "It isn't. I didn't want to cause friction between the two of you. But the list kept growing." He sighed and ran his hand through his jet-black hair.

"You didn't," I assured him. "I'm sure this won't be the last time Declan oversteps. I'm expecting it. And we'll deal with it every time it happens until it doesn't anymore."

"You're sure you …"

Inarus trailed off, and I nodded to his unspoken question. "I'm sure. We didn't have the best start, but we're here now. I know you don't approve." I paused and chewed my lower lip, hoping he would refute me, but he didn't.

"You don't need my approval. You're an adult."

I glared at him. "You kinda suck at being a friend, you know that?"

He nudged my shoulder. "Yeah, I'm a work in progress."

Well, at least he owned it.

Chapter Four

We drove through the Compound gates, our headlights illuminating the road before us. Two women stood at the front doors to the Compound.

"What the hell?" Declan broke off with a curse. He parked, slammed the door behind him, and stalked toward our unexpected guests.

I followed, though at a much slower and less threatening pace, and scrubbed a hand over my face. This wasn't going to be good.

"How did you get past my security?" Declan's voice was a thunderous roar.

I sighed. No "hello". No "thanks for coming". Nope, just right into questions and threats.

That really wasn't the best tone to take with the witches you wanted help from.

"And good evening to you, Declan. Miss Naveed."

I nodded toward Olivia Fields and gave her daughter, Marcella, a small wave.

She returned it, but when Declan took a threatening step forward, she shifted to hide behind her mother.

Annoyance thrummed through me. I smacked Declan on the shoulder. "Stop that. You're scaring her."

Declan scowled at me, but when I indicated the child, he took a deep breath and took two steps back.

Better.

"I'm sorry," he said to Marcella. "I mean you no harm. Your mother's visit is … unexpected." The last word came out as a growl.

She peeked out from behind her mother and gave him a wavering smile, her violet eyes still wide.

Declan crouched down to eye level with the thirteen-year-old girl.

"What brings you two here tonight?" he asked. His shoulders were relaxed, his expression friendly. I could still feel his agitation through the bond, but he was doing his best to temper it.

Declan had always had a way with children, but I'd assumed it only worked on shifter children. He had a way of making them feel safe and protected. Nothing could ever hurt them so long as he was around.

But seeing Marcella respond to him, I realized that his comforting presence wasn't exclusive to shifters.

Her smile broadened, and she moved to stand in front of him, her fear rapidly fading. She rubbed awkwardly at one arm before glancing at her mother for permission to speak.

Olivia nodded, and Marcella took a deep breath as though bracing herself. "My visions are getting worse. Mother and the others completed the spell work to bind your enemy ahead of schedule, but when they did …" she trailed off.

Worry coursed through me. Marcella was a hybrid child. Part witch, part psyker. Her abilities lay in the spectrum of a chronokinetic—a psyker capable of manipulating time. She hadn't grown into her abilities any further than seeing visions of the future. At least not that we knew of. But her visions were never good.

I only hoped that this time she didn't see visions of me destroying the city or anyone I cared about. I couldn't take the stress right now.

"What was it that you saw?" Declan placed a comforting hand on her shoulder.

Marcella leaned into the touch. "Blood." She paled. "I saw blood and death and pain. So much pain."

I worried my lower lip. *Please don't be about me.* Her last vision had seen me destroying the city and everyone I loved. I'd managed to change that future, but it had almost cost me my life.

"Whose?" he asked, his voice gentle.

I flicked my gaze toward Olivia. Her gray hair was pulled tight into a severe bun at her nape, highlighting the fine crisscross of scars that decorated her skin in an almost delicate pattern.

Olivia's eyes were solemn. "We don't know," she answered for her daughter. "Marcella only sees chaos and destruction. She's seen casualties on all sides across all five factions."

"All five?" Declan asked.

Marcella answered, "Shifter, Vampire, Human, Witch, and Psyker."

I scrunched my brows. Psykers had never been considered their own faction, though it made sense. "How do we stop it?" Whatever *it* was.

"We don't know, but the visions didn't begin until the spell work took hold in the binding. We think the woman is a catalyst of sorts."

"Did you bring it with you?" Declan asked.

Olivia nodded and pulled a thick silver cuff from her purse. It was three inches wide, maybe an eighth of an inch thick, and decorated with a scrollwork pattern.

"Once on the skin, the spell will activate, and it will mold to the wrist, making it virtually impossible to remove. This will keep the woman from accessing her powers. We don't know with certainty how long the magic will last, but we're confident it should last at least two weeks."

"What happens after two weeks?" I asked.

Olivia shrugged her shoulders. "If the magic wears off, then it will release itself. If the magic is still strong, then it won't. But once on, there isn't a way to remove it. Not that we've spent much time trying to counter our spell work to find out."

Declan took the cuff from Olivia and held it up for scrutiny. "You're sure it will work?"

Olivia smiled. "You're welcome to try it if you have any doubts."

That earned her a growl. "I'm not stupid," he told her.

"That is yet to be determined."

DECLAN STILL WASN'T happy that Olivia had gotten inside the Compound gates without his security noticing, and Brock—the werelion in charge of said security—wasn't any happier.

It was almost laughable.

Brock took a breach in security like a dagger to the heart. His cognac eyes were downcast as he tugged at the gold stud in his left ear, a determined look on his face. "I'll locate where the breach occurred. You have my word." His lips pressed together in a tight line, and he flicked a murderous glare in Olivia's direction.

"You could just ask her, you know," I suggested.

That earned me a cutting glare.

I raised both hands up. "Or not. You could totally do things the hard way, too. Whatever you think is best."

Brock spun on his heel and stalked down the hallway, not bothering to respond. I smothered a laugh before I turned to Declan, a wry grin on my face. "Was it something I said?"

He shook his head, but a small smile quirked his lips. "Olivia's enjoying this too much. Whatever she told us wouldn't be the truth. Assuming she told us anything at all. Brock is better off figuring it out on his own and then strengthening the perimeter to make sure it doesn't happen again."

I sighed but nodded. I wasn't thrilled with a security breach any more than he was, but we had a crazy-ass psyker to wake up, so with everything else on my plate, I'd let them worry about the breach.

I fingered the silver wrist cuff in my hands. The metal was cool to the touch but every few seconds it sent a *zing* through my fingertips. It reminded me of static shock. A quick zap that made you twitch but didn't hurt.

"Are you ready?"

"Am I a complete jerk for not calling Inarus and telling him what we're doing?"

I was. Dia was his sister, and he'd trusted me to watch over her while he took care of repairs and renovations at Sanborn Place.

Declan was quiet long enough that I looked up.

"If you're really thinking about it, then I am. Because you don't even like the guy and you realize it's an asshole move."

I handed him the cuff and pulled out my phone for what seemed like the hundredth time today.

Inarus answered on the first ring.

"The witches came up with a spell that will bind Dia's powers. We're getting ready to use it so we can wake her up. Can you step away?"

"I'll be right there."

The line went dead.

"He should be— " Before I could finish my sentence, Inarus stood in front of us.

Show off.

He ran a hand through his jet-black hair before shoving his hands into his front jean pockets. His blue-gray eyes were brighter than usual. "We need ground rules," he said.

"No one will hurt your sister."

Declan snorted behind me.

I peered over my shoulder and mouthed, "*Not helping*".

Not that Declan cared. If he'd had his way, Dia would be dead, and we'd have all moved on by now.

"Look, you're here, right? If we wanted to be assholes and do this behind your back, we could have. We're taking things one step at a time, and you'll be involved in each one."

Inarus didn't look convinced, but nodded.

"All right, then. Let's get this show on the road."

Chapter Five

The small room was cramped with so many bodies inside. Olivia and Marcella stood to the far left of the room. Inarus stood at Dia's right. Frankie and Annabeth—the Pack's resident healers—were stationed on Dia's immediate left, leaving Declan and I to stand at the foot of the bed.

Inarus placed the cuff on Dia's wrist and stepped back.

We all took a collective breath.

Nothing happened.

I flicked my eyes to Olivia and lifted a brow. *Wasn't something magical supposed to happen?*

She shrugged. "It's magic, not fireworks. What did you expect?"

I rolled my eyes. "I don't know. Something exciting, maybe?"

She snorted.

I moved closer to the bed. On first inspection, the cuff wasn't doing anything, but as I got closer, I realized that the cuff was moving like molasses along Dia's exposed flesh.

It shrank little by little, curving to the contours of her wrist.

Minutes ticked by. I tapped my foot, never taking my eyes off of the cuff lest I miss something. I scowled down at the shiny metal. *Any day now.*

I wasn't sure what I'd been expecting, but this hadn't been it.

After five full minutes, the cuff finally molded to her skin, leaving not even a hair's breadth between it and her flesh. I examined the cuff, tracing my finger along its edge. "Now wha—"

Light flared, and runes stood out in stark contrast along the surface.

I dropped her arm and took a step back as a bright light burst into the room, all but blinding me. It was gone as quickly as it'd come, and the runes it'd illuminated faded right along with it.

"Now you can wake her," Olivia said, her expression smug.

So much for no fireworks.

Frankie and Annabeth moved to remove Dia's feeding tube.

I turned, not needing to see the process. Something about a long tube coming out of someone's nose made me squeamish.

With that done, Frankie pulled a syringe from her medical coat pocket and turned toward Declan.

"The adrenaline should hit her system and cause her to wake almost instantly. She'll feel disoriented for a few seconds, but given that she's in good health, she should snap to pretty quick. Ready?"

He nodded.

I chewed my lower lip as Frankie connected the syringe to the IV port still in Dia's forearm, pushed the plunger, and stepped back.

"Y'all have fun. Frankie and I will leave you to your business," Annabeth said.

The two women strode out of the room, and not a second too soon.

Dia's eyes snapped to attention. In less than five seconds she'd catalogued the room. I tracked her eyes as they hit each one of us —Declan, Olivia, Marcella, Inarus, and then me.

When her eyes met mine, fury flashed through them, and she lunged from the bed like a wild cat.

Blankets flew, and before I realized what was happening, she plowed into me, throwing me flat on my back.

What the hell?

She wrapped her legs around my waist and her arms around my neck. My airway constricted, and we rolled across the ground.

I shoved my elbow back into her stomach and managed a brief gasp before her arms tightened again.

No one moved.

Inarus stood open mouthed as I struggled on the floor with his sister.

Marcella hid behind her mother, Olivia holding her arms back protectively to guard her daughter.

And Declan stood, eyes wide with a startled expression on his face.

If I weren't on the verge of suffocating, I would laugh at the look on his face.

"Little help here," I choked out.

I hunched my shoulders forward and tried to roll her off me, but she wasn't budging. The damn woman was like a spider monkey hanging on for dear life.

I elbowed her again, and that got me a punch in the head.

Stars clouded my vision, but I didn't miss Declan's normally green eyes flood with gold when she struck me.

I smacked Dia's arm, drawing her attention.

She scowled down at me, having the nerve to look annoyed, like I was some fly she wanted to swat.

Right back at you, twatwaffle.

"You really want to let me go now," I warned.

I'd managed to maneuver my body to the side so she was almost grasping my head to her chest in an embrace. A suffocating one, but at least I could get a good look at her now with my face angled up.

Her eyes narrowed, and her lips pressed into a thin line. She squeezed tighter.

Oh well. Your funeral.

Declan took a menacing step forward, and thankfully Inarus didn't make the mistake of trying to stop him. Though he clearly wanted to, judging by the lines of worry bracketing his mouth and the twitch in his hands.

I shook my head. *Please don't.*

"Release my mate, and I'll forget for the next ten minutes that I want to rend your flesh from your bones." His voice sent chills up my spine, and it wasn't even directed at me. I could only imagine what was going through Dia's head.

She didn't have a lot of options. By now she would have realized that she couldn't teleport out of the room, and while she was a fighter, she couldn't take on all of us.

And she sure as hell couldn't take on Declan.

I struggled against her hold and managed to get one hand beneath her arm and force it away from my neck.

Woohoo! Air.

"Last warning." Declan's skin rippled.

She released me, and I jerked forward on hands and knees.

Declan grabbed me and jerked me to my feet before he shoved me behind him.

I coughed and braced my hands on my knees as I gasped for breath.

"Good morning to you, too, *bitch.*" I rubbed at my neck, flinching when I touched a sore spot.

That was going to leave a bruise.

Dia climbed to her feet and reared backward. Her eyes frantically searched for an exit.

"Dia." Inarus strode forward with both hands lifted in surrender. "We just want to talk."

She sneered. "Traitor. I didn't believe them, but look at you."

She folded her arms across her chest and slid her feet back a few steps more, but she had nowhere to go.

Inarus flinched under her verbal assault, and I waited to see what he would do. This wasn't your typical family reunion. From what he'd told me, he hadn't seen his sister in three years.

She'd been eighteen when he left, living in Portland, Oregon. He hadn't wanted to involve her with the HAC, but she'd clearly managed to get herself involved all by her lonesome.

I didn't know if they'd been close before. Hell, until she showed up and tried to kill me, I hadn't even realized he had a sister.

But I could see from the look on his face that her opinion of him mattered. *Peachy.*

Having caught my breath, I stepped around Declan. He growled and tried to push me behind him again, but I wasn't having it.

"What the hell is your problem?" I spat.

Maybe if I riled her up some more, she'd direct all her hate and anger at me instead of Inarus.

And boy, did it work.

Dia lunged for me again. This time, Inarus caught her.

"You're my problem." She kicked and swung despite Inarus holding her back, eager to get to me.

Alrighty, then. It was going to be like that. I took three steps forward, and before I could convince myself it was a bad idea, I swung.

My fist connected with her jaw, and her head snapped back. Pain exploded in my knuckles, but I didn't care. I shook out my hand and smiled when her eyes rolled back in her head.

"Hah!"

Inarus' eyes widened, and Dia fell from his arms, hitting the floor with a solid thunk.

"Aria! What the hell?" Inarus fumbled to lift her back up.

"I've been wanting to do that all day." I looked down at my hand and wiggled my fingers. Nothing broken. *Phew.* "Besides, you're the one who dropped her."

Chapter Six

The witches left, and Declan and I retreated back to my room to give Inarus some time to cool down and get Dia settled back into bed.

We'd collectively agreed to sedate her and have a do-over in the morning.

Inarus wasn't thrilled that I'd hit his sister, but he was, thankfully, pretty understanding.

Okay, he was pissed that I'd sucker punched her while he was holding her back, but he was giving me a pass since she did try to kill me.

Twice now.

I rubbed my eyes and pulled the hair tie free from my hair.

Declan came up behind me and pulled my back flush against him. He fisted my hair in his hand and kissed the sensitive skin between my neck and shoulder.

"You're supposed to be going to bed," I reminded him, though I still tilted my head to the side, giving him better access.

His tongue traced the twin puncture marks on my neck—remnants of his bite when he'd claimed me.

I shivered.

"How am I supposed to go to bed without my mate beside me?" His voice was a rumbling growl that sent butterflies dancing through my stomach.

I rolled my eyes and turned to face him. "You agreed to the rule." I may not have given him much say in it, but he'd still consented.

His eyes hooded. "You said no sex. You didn't say you'd isolate yourself in a separate room and refuse to let me touch you."

I wasn't isolating myself.

Okay, maybe I was. But how else was I supposed to keep my hands off of him when he looked like *that*?

Six feet of hard, muscled flesh and the face of a Viking warrior. And when he did that growling thing …

I shook myself.

We were still getting to know one another. Sex would just complicate our already complicated relationship. We needed more time.

Gold flecks filled his gaze, and he reached for me once more.

Need echoed through the bond between us.

I allowed him to pull me close, feeling the hard ridges of his muscles against my softer flesh.

God, he would feel good naked against me.

Declan lifted a brow.

Shit. Did I say that out loud?

He captured my mouth with his, and before I could dwell on it, he slipped his tongue past my lips, eliciting a moan from me. I kissed him back and wrapped my arms around his neck. Pine and mint exploded along my senses. I wanted to envelop myself in his scent.

I needed to mark him.

Where the hell had that thought come from?

Tugging on the short strands of his white blond hair, I forced him back to catch my breath. "Rules," I panted.

"Screw the rules." Declan crushed his mouth against mine, and in a sweeping motion, lifted me into his arms and carried me toward the bed.

Despite his kiss being hot and full of tamped aggression, he laid me on the bed with infinite care.

His hands were firm but gentle. He caressed my leg, my hip, the side of my breast.

My body arched into his touch. I needed him. Needed more.

I bit down on my lower lip. I should stop this. But I didn't. Because dammit, I wanted him.

I pulled at the hem of Declan's shirt, and without needing any further encouragement, he pulled it off.

Sun-kissed skin met my gaze. I drank in the site of him hungrily.

My shirt followed seconds after.

A growl rumbled in Declan's chest and I suddenly forgot to breathe.

"God, you're so beautiful." He kissed me again.

Heat suffused me, and a tingling sensation broke out along my skin. I gasped for breath.

Declan reached for the waistband of my pants.

I'd never been so grateful for wearing yoga pants in my life. With a quick tug, they were dragged off and thrown to the floor.

I pushed him back.

Declan's eyes fell, concern etching lines between his eyebrows, but only for a second.

Sparks ignited in his gaze when, with shaking fingers, I unhooked his belt and pushed his jeans down over his narrow hips, taking his briefs with them.

He pounced, and I fell back.

His eyes were liquid gold now. I bit at his lower lip and took pleasure in the wanting that thrummed through our bond.

He kissed my neck, my jaw.

My own desires were magnified by his. It was exhilarating

and overwhelming all at once.

Sharp claws pressed against my skin, and fabric ripped as Declan slashed at my bra and then my underwear.

"Hey!" My complaint was cut short by another kiss.

"I'll buy you new ones."

I laughed. "You can't just shred my clothes whenever you feel like it," I told him, though my body seemed to like the idea.

"Watch me." Declan parted my knees, and for a moment, just stared down at me. His gaze roved over my body with open possession.

The ache between my legs intensified. I reveled in it. Something primal inside of me wanted to be his. To be possessed by him.

"Mine." His voice was gravelly and pure sex.

Then those lips, that delicious mouth, were on the sensitive skin of my inner thighs. His stubbled jaw scraped over my flesh.

Oh, God.

Declan kissed his way up my thighs to my heated core, and before I could stop him, he licked me in my most intimate area.

A purr of deep pleasure rumbled in his throat,

My back bowed, and I arched into his kiss. "Please—"

Declan was power and strength. His eyes gleamed wickedly as he gazed up my body from his position near my core. He kissed me again.

God, yes.

My head tossed and turned.

"Look at me."

He pulled back, enough for me to see the moisture now gleaming on his seductive lips.

"Please what?"

"I need you."

"No more rules?"

I shook my head. *Fuck the rules.* I wanted him, needed him inside of me. Now.

Declan rose and leaned over me. He braced his hands on either side of my head. "Are you sure?"

"Dammit, Declan. Fuck me." I inwardly cringed.

I hadn't meant for it to come out that way, but it was getting harder to think clearly past the arousal and nerves.

Declan didn't seem to mind. He tilted my head back and kissed me full on the mouth. His lips were demanding, and his erection pressed against my entrance.

There was something erotic about tasting myself on his tongue. I whimpered into his kiss as one of his hands cupped my bare breast. Sensation prickled through every one of my nerve endings to pool between my legs.

Fire broke out along my skin.

Shit.

Declan jerked back.

"Sorry." I covered my face, mortified.

"Hey." Declan pulled my hand away and kissed my nose before resting his head against mine.

"Just breathe." He fondled my breast and rolled one taut nipple between his fingers.

"Not helping."

He smiled like a cat that'd caught the canary.

I sucked in breath after breath and tried to calm my racing heartbeat.

"There you go. That's my girl."

His girl? I liked how that sounded.

The flames receded, and Declan gripped my jaw and kissed me again like nothing had happened.

He was going to drive me to edge of insanity if he kept kissing me like that. I bit down on his lower lip.

"Fuck!"

Less than a second after that one word, I found my legs wrapped around Declan's waist as he positioned himself at my opening and pressed into me in a single fluid thrust.

He filled me so completely, I cried out his name.

He pulled out, and this time thrust into me slower, deeper.

My head fell back, then I sank my nails into his shoulders and buried my face into his chest. *Good. So good. Needed—*

"More—"

Declan didn't need to be told twice. His pace increased, steadily pounding into me. He was deep, relentless, and ruthlessly fast.

His chest rubbed against my sensitive nipples with every thrust.

I rocked beneath him, and wave after wave of pleasure built inside of me.

I clung to him tighter.

Declan reached down between our bodies. His fingers moved expertly over my clit, and I exploded. My body clenched beneath him. The bed shook. Pleasure rolled through me like a violent wave.

It was as if the entire room shuddered with my release, leaving me boneless beneath him.

Declan kissed me and increased his tempo. His driving need built inside of me, and I felt the sharp bite of his orgasm just before he came.

We both cried out again.

"Love you. So good." The words came out a growl.

My body gripped him as he pulsed inside of me. I felt taken. Possessed. Owned.

And I liked it.

Declan shifted beside me and pulled me against his chest, tucking my head beneath his chin.

He stroked my bare shoulder, and I made small circles in the thin dusting of hair on his broad chest.

"You are my heart." He kissed the top of my head.

Contentment filled me.

Chapter Seven

The quiet never lasted. The incessant knocking on my bedroom door was indication enough of that truth.

I stretched my arms above my head and moved to get up and see who it was, when Declan wrapped an arm around my waist and pulled me closer against his bare chest.

"Mmm … not yet." His voice was a seductive growl in my ear that sent shivers down my spine.

Images of last night flooded my consciousness. His kiss. His touch. I sighed. This felt good. It felt right.

And there was that knocking again.

Declan growled. "Who is coming to your room at"—he peered over my shoulder to look at the alarm clock—"six in the morning?"

I groaned. Six meant I'd only slept maybe four hours.

"I don't know, but it's probably important." Shifters tended to keep odd hours. They stayed up late and slept well into the double digits.

I threw the blankets off and squeaked when I realized I'd fallen asleep naked.

Declan reached out a hand to capture my hip and tugged me close before I could cover myself.

"You're beautiful." He nuzzled my hair and boldly cupped my breast.

The knocking persisted.

Ugh. "Let me see if it's important."

He scowled, but released me and folded his arms behind his head. His emerald eyes tracked me as I ran across the room and slipped into his discarded T-shirt and he made a sound of appreciation in the back of his throat. One I chose to ignore.

The shirt fell to just above my knees.

Another knock.

"I'm coming!" I called and swung the door open.

Inarus stood on the other side of the door. His hair was mussed, his clothes were rumpled, and his blue-gray eyes were wild.

Shit. Something had happened.

"She's gone."

I froze, but only for a second. "What do you mean she's gone?"

He ran his fingers through his jet-black hair and paced in front of me. "I mean she's gone. I left her for five minutes to use the bathroom. She was unconscious. It shouldn't have mattered that I left. But when I came back, her bed was empty."

He placed his hands on either one of my shoulders and stared into my eyes. "It was only five minutes."

His gaze implored me to believe him. And I did.

Inarus wouldn't have spirited her away. At least, I really hoped he wouldn't have.

I looked over my shoulder to see Declan already out of bed and dressed in his jeans. He pulled his phone from his pocket and made a call, but I couldn't hear who he was speaking with. It didn't take a genius to guess it was likely Brock, the Pack's Head of Security.

I turned my attention back to Inarus. "Get to the main entrance and trace your way back to her room. After that, check the perimeter. She couldn't have gone far since she can't port."

He nodded, but worry filled his gaze as he stared over my shoulder in Declan's direction. "If anyone else finds her—"

"They'll use minimal and non-lethal force only. You have my word."

His lips pressed into a thin line, but he nodded.

"Go."

Inarus bolted down the hall toward the staircase that would lead him to the main floor and the main entrance. He could have ported there, but then he'd miss the chance to intercept her.

Dia didn't know the layout of the Compound. It was a series of interconnected hallways in a seventy-four thousand square foot building made up of six floors that had been configured like a maze. Being human without a shifter's keen sense of smell, I knew just how easy it was to get lost in here.

With any luck, we'd find Dia soon. Before she could cause too much trouble.

I closed the door behind me and made quick work of getting dressed. I threw on a pair of faded blue jeans and a gray cotton shirt that said, "My blood type is coffee."

"Brock's been informed, and all the nurseries are on lockdown. We won't risk her going after the children."

The children.

Worry gnawed at my gut. Had that been the plan all along?

Inarus and I had rescued seven shifter children from the clutches of the HAC. Had Dia allowed herself to be captured to get inside the Compound and get them back?

I shook my head. *No.* That wasn't possible. Because Dia's aim had never been capture. She'd been trying to kill me. And she'd almost succeeded the first time around.

"Inarus is going to check the front entrance and the perimeter …" I paused as I waited for Declan to meet my gaze.

He looked up after shoving his phone into his back pocket. "I promised him we would use nonlethal force."

Declan's upper lip curled. "If she—"

"I promised." I kept my eyes locked on his. After a few seconds he nodded, but he didn't look happy about it. "If she has harmed any of our people, there will be consequences."

I smiled. He'd said "ours".

Not waiting a moment longer, we left the room in search of Inarus' sister. We didn't want to cause panic or alert Dia to our search, so we looked for her quietly. Brock had all the Pack's sentries on high alert, but we kept the hallways free of added soldiers. No need to sound the alarm.

Fifteen minutes later we'd turned up nothing.

"Dammit." I shook my head. "Where the hell could she have gone?" I was scratching the back of my head as Declan pushed open the double doors to the commons area, and we both came to a screeching halt.

"What the—"

Across from us was Dia, seated in a leather lounge chair with a coffee table between her and her companion, Robert Yazzie, Alpha to Clan Canidae.

"Damn coyote." Declan stalked forward.

I quickened my steps to keep up, and saw Robert's wicked smile when he caught sight of us heading his direction. As a coyote shifter, he benefited from what most shapeshifters did. Lean bodies, sculpted muscles, and a glint in their eyes that would make any human swoon.

Robert was also devilishly handsome. Perfect lines, a cut jaw, blond hair, and startling blue eyes.

I had to remind myself not to let his good looks fool me, because he was still—as Declan said—a damn coyote.

And one hell of a sneaky bastard at that.

Before Declan could say anything, I placed a hand on his bicep and smiled in Robert's direction. "We were just looking for you." I flicked my gaze toward Dia, who glowered at me. "Would you mind if we borrowed him for just a moment?"

There was probably too much pep in my voice, but it couldn't be helped. Full of sunshine and rainbows wasn't my style, and it showed.

She nodded curtly and took a drink from her mug, her attention now anywhere but on me.

"Robert?" I gave him my hard stare. The one that said *do not fuck with me and get your ass out of that chair. Now.*

He stood. "Of course. I'll only be a moment." He bent and kissed her hand before following us a short distance away.

I didn't miss the blush that crept up her cheeks. *Interesting.*

When we were out of earshot, Declan did as expected. He let Robert have it.

"Of all the reckless things you could have done." Agitation had his muscles bunching beneath his shirt. "Do you have any idea who that woman is? The threat she poses to our entire Pack?" His tone was full of fury and indignation and his anger pressed against the mate bond sparking my own irritation.

I tangled my fingers with his.

He didn't acknowledge the action with words, but his hand squeezed mine in a show of thanks.

Robert's brows creased, and a tick formed in his jaw. "She was wandering the hallways without an escort. What did you expect me to do? Would you have preferred I attack, put her on the defensive, and thereby seal our fates in her eyes as the enemy?" He kept his tone even as he spoke.

Smart. Declan was on edge, and Robert knew he didn't have much rope left with which to hang himself.

As Declan chewed on Robert's words, I intrejected, "What have you two been talking about? Did she say anything about the attack or the HAC?"

Robert shook his head and shoved his hands into his jean pockets. "We hadn't gotten that far. My goal was to make her comfortable. Not interrogate her. She needs an ally here. She has enough enemies."

I narrowed my gaze. "You're manipulating her?" I shouldn't have been surprised. And if I was honest, I was impressed.

Robert's smile was full of menace and wicked adulation. "Would you expect anything else from me?"

No. But … "She isn't some toy for you to—"

He lifted a hand, silencing me.

Declan growled, and Robert took a small step back.

"I meant no offense." Declan quieted enough that Robert continued, "I'm aware she is not a toy. She is the enemy. Your enemy. I will do what is necessary to ensure the safety of my people. If that means toying with one lonely human's heart, so be it."

He stalked away and left us staring at his retreating back as he retook his seat across from Dia.

She smiled warmly at him.

She was so screwed.

"She … likes him." The damn coyote was infuriating most of the time, insufferable the rest. Yet, he'd somehow wormed his way under her defenses.

"It would seem so," Declan grumbled. "I'll have Brock call off the search. I doubt Dia can trick our trickster. We'll give them time, and see how this pans out."

Chapter Eight

Inarus wasn't thrilled when I told him where his sister was, but he agreed to leave them be.

For now.

He returned to Sanborn Place to continue managing repairs. With any luck we'd be back in business by week's end.

The Compound teemed with activity. We had a guest, and everyone wanted to know her purpose. Who she was and how she'd ended up here was at the forefront of everyone's mind. Shifters had always been secretive, and prior to me, outsiders had never been welcome within the Compound.

Hell, I still wasn't welcomed by everyone, and I was mated to their Alpha.

But the interest in Dia hadn't yet turned hostile. Though we couldn't expect that to last. The Clan Alphas had already begun pressing Declan to do something. They were overwhelmed with clan-mate questions and had no answers to give them.

Someone would crack.

Declan walked up behind me and wrapped his arms around me.

For a brief moment I stiffened, but the heady scent of pine

and mint that was unique to him had me relaxing into his embrace.

He nuzzled my neck, and I took comfort in his touch. He was warm. Safe.

But a part of me still rejected the notion. It was dangerous to get close to him. To get close to anyone. It would only put him at risk. If it wasn't Marcella's visions, then it was my mother.

There was always something.

"You're worried."

It wasn't a question, but I nodded my head in answer anyway, unsurprised that he'd picked up on my emotions. "Dia is the catalyst to what could be our end, and she's walking the halls like she owns them. Of course, I'm worried."

Declan bit down on the sensitive skin between my neck and shoulder with blunt teeth. I shivered. He laved at the skin he'd marked, and then kissed my temple.

"Robert is a strategist. It's why he rose to be his Clan's Alpha. Trust him."

I snorted. "Trust the trickster?"

Declan laughed. "I know how it sounds, but yes. Robert and I grew up side by side. We've always been rivals, but despite our differences, he has earned my trust. He will earn yours."

I worried my lower lip as nerves ate at my stomach. "I just keep waiting for the next bomb to go off."

He fell quiet. "You've been through a lot. Have you spoken to anyone?"

I shook my head. "No."

"You should talk to somebody. We have three therapists on the Pack's payroll right now. Any one of them would be happy to help."

Not happening. "I'm fine."

Declan sighed and turned me to face him. He cupped my face in his calloused palms. "You're not fine. The ground is shaking."

I scowled, and then realized that tiny tremors racked the room. *Dammit.* I closed my eyes and concentrated. The tremors ceased.

"See, I'm fine."

"Aria, you've been through a lot this year alone. The mother you thought was dead came back into your life only for you to realize she'd abandoned you. You almost died during a battle with a Chupacabra. You were forced ..." He trailed off, and I reached up on tiptoe to press my lips against his.

He returned the gesture, but only for a moment before pulling away. "I know you didn't ask for this. It's been an adjustment. If you still resented me, I wouldn't blame you—"

"Stop. I don't. We are the one thing that's good in my world right now." We still had a lot to figure out. But being with Declan felt right. I wasn't going to deny that feeling any longer.

He smiled, but it didn't reach his eyes. Declan tucked a loose strand of hair behind my ear and rested his forehead against mine. "You've been attacked more times than I can count. Abducted. Experimented on. You should talk to somebody. It will help."

"I'll think about it," I told him.

"That's all I ask." He captured my lips with his once more. "If Caden or one of the other children you'd rescued came to you with concerns, what would you tell them to do?"

I sighed. "It isn't the same. They were kidnapped and tortured by the HAC."

Declan met my gaze and waited.

Fine, they were the same. But my mind rebelled at the thought of exposing myself to a virtual stranger. It wouldn't help. Talking never did.

I knew what *would* help.

I needed to kill my mother and dismantle the HAC piece by piece. After watching her emotionless eyes look down on me as I was strapped down to a cold metal table and had my psyker energy ripped apart inside of me, I'd realized in that moment that she needed to die.

I'd come to terms with that truth over the last few weeks.

I still didn't know if I could actually do it. She'd raised me. She'd brushed my waist-length hair every night before bed, kissed my cheek, and told me she loved me for years. The small child inside of me still loved her with every fiber of my being.

But she was the head of the proverbial snake.

There were no signs of the mother I grew up loving anymore. She'd died six years ago.

"Christian believes the work will be completed by week's end," I said.

Declan didn't comment on my change of subject.

"I could use a gig right now to get my mind off of things and get out of the Compound. I'm beginning to develop cabin fever."

"You don't need to work. You—"

I lifted my hand. "I need to work. I need to be independent. We had an agreement."

"We still do. I only want you to know that you have choices. You don't have to put yourself in danger to have independence."

"I like what I do. I help people." My work wasn't always rewarding. Bodyguard duty for a water nymph or retrieving lost genetically manipulated pets weren't the gigs I was most proud of.

But keeping families safe. Eliminating the monsters. *That* I was proud of.

Declan's phone buzzed in his pocket. He pulled it out and stared down at the screen. A furrow formed between his brows.

I peered over to see what he was looking at.

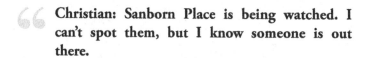

Christian: Sanborn Place is being watched. I can't spot them, but I know someone is out there.

Declan typed a quick response.

Declan: How long have you felt them?

Christian: The last two hours. Bobby wants to go take a look around outside.

Declan: Don't engage. I'll be right there.

"Christian thinks someone is spying on them. I'm going to go check things out." Declan shoved his phone into his pocket.

"If something is going on at Sanborn Place, I should be the one checking things out. Besides, you're Alpha. If anyone is there, they'll get sight of you and head for the hills before you have the chance to pick up their scent."

"The same applies to you. You won't have any more luck showing up without whoever is out there spotting you either."

He had a point.

"I'll send Inarus. He can port in and out unseen. He can also evacuate everyone inside if the need arises. Your men will be safe, and he'll have an easier time spotting whoever it is that's being an idiot and sleuthing around my business."

He nodded. "Do it."

Chapter Nine

Olivia had called earlier today and relayed a message from Marcella.

"The TK has to die."

She couldn't tell me which TK it was, only that Marcella had had a vision and that a TK needed to die in order for me to live. Inarus was a telekinetic. As was Dia. But It wasn't like I was going to kill either of them, so I decided to ignore Marcella's warning.

It wasn't helpful and only worked to dampen my mood. So, I decided to push the thought far from my mind. I busied myself training, and focused on the fight at hand.

It was an unfair fight, but beggars couldn't be choosers.

I would have preferred to spar with Declan. It was rare when he didn't hold back, but there were brief moments when I wormed my way under his skin just enough to force his control to slip. In those moments, his beast would rise to the surface and then things really got interesting. He pushed me to be at my best.

Today, I had Caden.

At seventeen years old, he was still slender and growing too fast. He'd passed six feet and was still going. Bright cognac eyes and sculpted cheekbones hinted at the masculine beauty he would inherit. He would give girls a reason to chase him should he ever look in their direction.

But as a recent addition to the Pack—having been rescued from the HAC—Caden only ever seemed to have one goal in mind. Grow stronger.

I couldn't blame him.

I pulled my daggers from the sheaths resting low on my hips.

Caden raised a single brow, and claws inched their way from his fingertips. At seventeen, he shouldn't have been able to manage a partial shift. But Caden was older than his years and full of surprises.

"I'll go easy on you," I told him.

He smirked. "I'd rather you didn't."

I whirled my blades, warming up my wrists.

Caden assumed a warrior's stance, and I lunged.

My blade whistled past his left side. He sidestepped my maneuver, dodged my charge, and shoved me between my shoulder blades.

I whirled back just enough to avoid the prick of his claws.

Ducking low, I kicked out, landing a blow to his right kneecap. His stance faltered, but only for a moment before he righted himself.

"You're getting better." Only a few weeks ago that move would have taken him to his knees.

"I'm a quick study."

Caden lunged. With the speed only a vampire or shifter could master, his clawed fingers sank into my shoulders, and he threw me to the mat.

I smelled blood.

Gold glinted in Caden's eyes. His beast scented prey.

Not today, buddy.

Recognizing that Caden was still too young, his beast still untrained, I ended the match before the blood overruled his senses.

I rolled to my feet and rammed the hilt of my dagger into his temple while my knee connected with his gut.

He sucked in a pained gasp, but didn't go down.

Definitely getting stronger.

I twisted and issued a roundhouse kick while he was still dazed, and he toppled over like a leaning tower.

His chest rose and fell in a steady rhythm as he lay on the mat.

I crouched down beside him and waited for his vision to clear and for his gaze to sharpen on me.

"Your control slipped. Your lion smelled blood, and you let it take over. He's stronger than you are, but you need the man's mind to take down a more experienced opponent."

He nodded. "It won't happen again."

"See that it doesn't."

I sheathed my blades and grabbed a towel from a nearby bench.

Caden was slow to get up, so I wiped the sweat from my brow and stretched out the aches in my neck and shoulders.

"Hey, Aria ..." His voice was hesitant.

"Yes?"

"You've killed before, right?"

I nodded. Where was he going with this?

"Does it follow you? The stain of death?"

I shook my head. "I only kill if I have to. I kill to protect myself, and I kill to protect others. I don't kill for sport, and I don't kill lesser creatures that don't know any better unless I'm given no choice. At the end of the day, I can look at myself in the mirror. Have a purpose behind your kills, and you'll be able to look yourself in the eye when you see your reflection too."

He nodded, but worry still marked his expression.

"What's this all about?"

Golden eyes met mine. "James is gone."

"He won't be gone forever." As Pack Hunter, Declan couldn't

afford for him to be gone much longer. He was dealing with Pack business. I didn't know what exactly, and I had enough on my plate to worry about, so I chose to remain ignorant.

It was easier than worrying about my best friend.

"Declan pulled me aside last week. Before you were hurt ..." He averted his gaze, and my own concern rose to the surface.

"What did he talk to you about?"

"He told me I'm Hunter-born."

Ah, all of this made sense now. "And how do you feel about that?"

Being Hunter-born was both a blessing and a curse. James had been the Pack's Hunter since the age of eighteen. The Hunter took down rogue shifters. It was a lonely occupation, and he had a hard time building relationships within the Pack for fear he'd one day have to end a friend's life.

If Caden was hunter-born, he'd be expected to kill rogues one day, too.

Lycanthropy, or Lyc-V for short, was a vicious virus that infected without discrimination. But because of its aggressive nature, it pushed a shifter's humanity to its limits and forced them to choose: Humanity, with all of its razor-thin control. Or release, and the freedom to let the beast take over.

Nearly one in every twenty shifters turned rogue.

It was why a Hunter was so important to the health of any Pack. Because only a Hunter was strong enough and dominant enough to challenge any Pack-mate—Alpha or otherwise—and not have their own beasts shaking with the urge to submit.

Caden still hadn't answer my question, so I waited.

And then my patience snapped, because let's be honest, I didn't have much to begin with. "Could you kill to protect those you loved?"

"Yes."

"Could you kill to protect those weaker than you?"

"Yes."

"If faced with killing someone you know, someone you may have once considered a friend or family, could you do it if you knew sparing their life would end Suzie, Tito's, Yuli's, or any of the other children's lives who came to the Pack when you did?"

He paused and considered the question before answering. "Yes."

"Then don't let the weight of being Hunter-born consume you. When a shifter goes rogue, there's no coming back."

"I know, it's just that ..."

It's just that having no choice but to kill a friend had the tendency to kill your soul.

I could relate. But telling Caden that slaying his friend when the time came would in fact leave him marked wasn't going to help him.

Nothing I said could. So I weaved a pretty lie with enough truth that he wouldn't scent it.

"Death is never easy. Neither is life. The Hunter does their Pack-mates a service by ending their life when they have lost the very essence of who they once were. The Hunter grants them peace. Would you deny them that?"

He shook his head.

"Then embrace your burden and train. James is still here, so the mantle of Hunter won't fall on your shoulders any time soon. Take advantage of the time you have to grow in both strength and confidence."

"Thanks. I needed that."

I walked over to him and ruffled his unkempt hair. "I like to think I give a mean pep talk."

Chapter Ten

D inner was a private affair. Shifters craved companionship, and mealtime was a time to socialize. But tonight, easy camaraderie and conversation weren't what was on the menu.

Seated in one of the Compound's private dining rooms were Robert, Dia, Derek and Teagan—Joint Alphas of Clan Wolf— Caden, Brock, Declan, and myself.

Brock was here at Declan's request. Caden at mine. And Derek and Teagan had invited themselves when they realized that Dia and Robert were joining us.

The brothers didn't want to miss out on any of the action. Not that I could blame them.

We each were seated around a rectangular table with Declan at the head, me on his right, Brock on his left, the rest of our party seated around us, and Dia seated farthest away.

It was for her own safety.

Inarus was still at Sanborn Place. Beneath the table, I typed a quick text. It had been several hours since I'd heard from him.

I wasn't one to worry. He was a telekinetic. He could take care of himself. But not checking in was unlike him, and I was curious to see what he'd discovered.

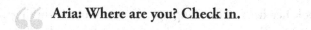 **Aria: Where are you? Check in.**

Putting my phone aside, I focused my attention on Robert and lifted a brow. He didn't seem to get the hint and continued on with his private conversation with Dia.

Declan's ears twitched, but there was no other indication that he was listening in on their conversation.

Dammit. I wished I had shifter hearing.

I checked the clock on the wall. It was six forty-eight, and time moved too slow.

Declan bit into his steak, and suddenly everyone at the table was ravenous. We ate in silence with only the sound of clinking silverware to fill the empty room.

I sent furtive glances in Dia's direction. Each one she met with a cold stare. *Right back atcha.* I wasn't going to be the one to break the silence, so I ate with a single-minded focus.

Caden was the one to speak first, surprising all of us.

"Were you involved in my abduction?"

Shit. I hadn't seen that coming.

Judging by the expression on Declan's face, neither had he.

"Perhaps we could entertain lighter dinner conversation—" Robert suggested.

I wanted to punch him in the teeth. Caden had been through a lot. This might not be the most comfortable setting, but he was owed answers.

Dia pushed her plate aside and leaned back in her chair. She met Caden's gaze straight on.

Gold flecks filled his eyes, but he made no move or sound. He waited. I could all but see his lion pacing just beneath the surface.

"That depends. When were you abducted?"

"Thirteen months and eleven days ago."

Damn. I hadn't realized he'd been keeping track.

Dia shook her head. "Too long ago. I've only been working with the HAC for the past six months after learning my brother had gone AWOL."

"So you didn't participate in mine, but you have in others?"

Dia glowered. "I didn't say that."

Caden's skin rippled.

I reached out and placed a hand on the bare skin of his left arm. He didn't look my way, but the touch grounded him, and his skin settled.

"Look, I'm a soldier. I was enlisted in the United States Army when society fell. I take orders. I don't ask questions. The HAC has given me plenty of orders, and I've followed every one of them. But I was never involved in assignments involving children. Are we good?"

Hardly. But we all waited to see what Caden would say.

He didn't disappoint.

"No. We're not good. You are my enemy. If you hurt any of mine, I will end you. I don't care if you think you're more experienced or stronger than I am. You're not. If you attack Aria again or harm anyone in my Pack, I will kill you. I won't think twice about it. Do we understand each other?"

Whoa.

Dia's lips pressed into a thin, white line. Seconds ticked by, and she finally nodded.

Caden pushed his chair back and stood. "With respect, I will excuse myself now."

Declan nodded, and Caden left the room.

If tensions were thick before, they were suffocating now.

"Dia has no intentions of attacking our Pack. Isn't that right?" Robert said in an attempt to ease the tension.

"No." She tried for a smile, but it didn't quit fit. "Previous altercations were just a misunderstanding."

I choked on the piece of steak I'd been chewing. "A

misunderstanding? Trying to kill me was a misunderstanding?" I fought the urge to rub at my neck.

She nodded. "I was under the impression you were manipulating my brother. I held you personally responsible for his standing within our organization."

Wonderful. "So, what was your plan? Kill me, and big bro would get his place back in the HAC, and then all would be well in the world?" I snorted. "They tried to kill him. More than once. You should be thanking me for getting him out of there."

She rose from her seat, palms spread on the table as she glared at me. "They never would have come after him if it weren't for you."

I stood, and fire licked my fingertips. "They didn't attack him because of me. They attacked him because he saved children. Children! They had kids locked in cages as they abused and experimented on them. What was he supposed to do, let them rot?"

"The HAC isn't perfect. But Viola is trying—"

"NO!" The room shook, and Dia flinched as if she'd been struck. Power filled my voice. My hair floated around me, and fire licked higher up my arms, encasing my upper body. "You do not get to bring my mother into this."

Her eyes widened. "Your mother?"

She had to be kidding. How could she not have known?

I laughed. The sound echoed in the room. I felt Declan's concern through the bond and ignored it. "You didn't know? Viola Reynolds is my mother."

Dia's eyes were the size of saucers. "But she—"

"Sent you to kill me?"

She swallowed hard and nodded.

"Dear old Mom doesn't like what doesn't fit perfectly in her plans. A psyker daughter is a pesky inconvenience."

Dia didn't say anything for several moments. The weight of the stares in my direction were making my skin itch.

I sat back down, took another bite of my steak and chewed as I worked on reducing my powers to a more manageable level.

"I'm sorry."

"Don't be. I don't need your pity."

"That isn't what I—"

"That's enough." Declan interjected, and all eyes turned in his direction.

I was grateful for his interruption, and I knew he'd done it for my benefit. "I have some questions, and I believe I'm owed those answers."

With a last flick of her gaze in my direction, Dia nodded and resumed her seat.

"Ask them."

"Why did you attack Aria at Sanborn Place?"

"I was given orders to capture or kill. She was marked as a threat to our mission."

Not surprising.

"And what is that mission?"

"Restoring social order and giving the power back to the people."

Declan growled beside me. "And what *people* might you be referring to?"

"Humans."

She was being oddly compliant. I looked at Robert, and got a grin out of him. Either he'd managed some serious schmoozing, or she was lying to us.

But if she were lying, every shifter in the room would have scented it and called her out.

"Where do your personal feelings lie in relation to your mission?"

Dia glowered at me. "I wanted to secure my brother's safety. I was told if I brought Aria in, they would stop hunting him."

Her reasoning was solid. If I'd been her, I would have done whatever I had to to protect the person I loved.

That didn't mean I was okay with her trying to kill me, though.

"Will you make additional attempts to capture or kill my mate?"

Wasn't that the million-dollar question?

Dia took a bite of her food and chewed. Stalling. She didn't want to answer, which was answer enough. "I won't make an attempt on her life so long as my brother's safety and well-being are secured."

Declan mulled that over.

"Do you believe the HAC will stop their manhunt if you deliver Aria to them?"

"No."

Well at least she wasn't a complete idiot.

"Will my word that your brother will remain unharmed so long as he is within these walls assure you of his safety?"

She flicked a glance to Robert.

He nodded. He'd prepared her for this conversation and likely told her this was as good as it was going to get. Declan didn't like Inarus. If it weren't for me, he'd have already given him the boot.

Inarus didn't live in the Compound on a permanent basis, but since he'd been staying in the apartment above Sanborn Place and the building was under repair, he'd started bunking with Caden.

Inarus' proximity had chafed Declan's tiger from day one.

"I want this removed." She lifted her arm and displayed the spellworked cuff.

"No. You're untrusted. Earn my trust, and it will be considered. But until then, it stays on."

Robert's nose twitched, scenting the lie. We couldn't take the cuff off. It fell off when the magic wore off, but Robert didn't need to know that, and he wasn't fool enough to call out his Alpha.

She chewed her lower lip. "Fine. We have an agreement."

"Good." Declan resumed his meal.

Teagan and Brock were the first to leave, followed closely by Dia and Robert.

Declan pulled my chair out and took my hand. It was a little after seven, but I was already ready for a hot shower and my bed.

"Aria, a moment?" Derek called out.

Declan lifted a brow.

"I'll be fine."

He nodded, but didn't look happy about it.

"Have a care with my mate," Declan warned.

Derek placed a hand over his heart. "On my honor."

Satisfied, Declan left.

When the room was empty, Derek closed the door behind him and resumed his seat.

Ah. Positioning himself lower than me so as not to be a threat. I might not be a shifter, but I understood them well enough.

I took the seat across from him and folded my hands in front of me.

"You're too trusting of the Coyote."

"I like to think I give everyone just enough rope to hang themselves with."

Derek considered that. "Declan is happy. You make him happy."

I waited. I didn't have a response to that. My relationship with Declan had been rocky up until recently, but it was our business and ours alone.

"On the surface, Robert supports your relationship. But did you ever wonder why he went against his Alpha and told you his failings?"

When I first met Declan, he'd wanted to use me. He thought by ensuring I was emotionally invested in someone within the

Pack that I'd be more amenable to coming to the Pack's aid should they need it.

He'd encouraged Pack-mates to court me. And then, he'd mate-claimed me against my will. I'd been dying, and there hadn't been an alternative to save my life. Claiming me had been the only viable option.

We were past that now, but the betrayal had run deep.

And when I'd accused him of taking advantage of his position, of still having an ulterior motive, Robert had been quick to lay stones at Declan's feet.

I hadn't given it much thought at the time, but looking back, I should have.

"Robert isn't your friend, and he can't be trusted. On the surface, he supports your relationship with Declan because it brings stability to the Pack. But in his eyes, you're a bad match. Any shifter in the Pack is a better choice than you. It has nothing to do with you as a person. I think Robert is actually fond of you. But he is closed-minded, and he doesn't trust outsiders. No matter how long you're here, you'll always be an outsider. That fact can't be helped. You're not a shifter and correct me if I'm wrong, but you can't become one, either?"

I shook my head. "I don't know. But I don't plan on finding out."

The Lycanthropy virus, or Lyc-V for short, was a virulent bitch that attacked the body on a genetic level. It mutated DNA and tainted the host's blood. But as much as it took, it gave. Speed, heightened senses, strength, and the inability to contract common diseases were just a handful of the benefits. In short, it was a disease. But no shifter would ever tell you they wanted a cure.

I, however, was happy as I was. I was both pyrokinetic and telekinetic. I didn't need anything else raging inside of me. My plate was already full.

Derek nodded. "I can respect that. But understand that most of the Pack will take issue with it and use it as a means to push you out. Robert would never attack you. Nor would he challenge you. But if you die, he will dance on your grave and shove the next available shifter under Declan's nose. Those two have a history. They were once like brothers, but something happened."

I opened my mouth to ask what, but he lifted a hand, halting my question.

"I don't know what caused them to drift apart, but I do know that while Robert has always put the good of the Pack first, he has also always found a way to get under Declan's skin and screw him. I trust that where Dia is concerned, he won't make any mistakes that put the Pack at risk. But if she slips her leash and kills you, I don't see him stepping in to help you."

I digested that. "Isn't my death detrimental to the Pack? If I die, there is a good chance Declan would too because of our bond."

He nodded. "There is that possibility. But Declan is strong, the strongest Alpha we've had in my lifetime. There is a chance he could survive your death. It's slim, but possible. There is also the matter of Robert's ambition. He rose to Clan Alpha around the same time Declan rose to become Alpha of Clan Cat. Robert plots and schemes. It wouldn't surprise me if he'd had his eyes set on becoming the Pack Alpha, but Declan beat him to the punch. If Robert had moved first, there's a chance Declan wouldn't have challenged him, just as Robert won't challenge Declan now. Their strength and dominance are too evenly matched, and both men are qualified in their roles. But with Declan out of the picture …" He let the statement hang.

"Then he could step into the position he truly wants." I sighed and stared down at the wooden table, tracing a knot with my fingertip. "Declan trusts Robert." Hell, earlier today, he'd told me to trust him. "But I appreciate the warning. I'll keep it in mind when Robert and I come into contact with one another."

Derek stood and left the room. As a man of few words, he'd sure as hell given me a lot to think about.

Chapter Eleven

I paced the confines of Declan's room.

"I need to go check on Inarus."

There. I said it.

I braced myself for Declan's reaction.

He leaned back on the headboard of his four-poster bed. His eyes hooded as he tracked my movements. "He's fine. Come to bed."

No anger. That was good.

I usually did my best to ignore the mate bond that connected us. It could be a royal pain trying to separate his feelings from my own, but right now, all I felt was a sea of my own anxiety and a hint of Declan's calm.

I rubbed at my arms. "Something feels off. Have you talked to Christian?"

He sighed. "I don't make it a habit of micromanaging my people."

Good to know. I'd make sure to remind him of that if he ever tried to micromanage me.

"I'm going to call him." I pulled out my phone and dialed Inarus' number.

Voicemail.

I tried the office number.

Voicemail.

Shit.

I threw my phone on the bed and ran my hands through my hair.

"Do you want me to call Christian?"

I nodded. "Please."

Declan exhaled a long-suffering sigh. I knew he thought I was overreacting, but something in me told me I wasn't.

He dialed Christian's number into his phone and then scowled.

"What?"

"Voicemail."

"Can you call any of the other workers?"

He nodded and dialed.

After several tense seconds, he shook his head.

Dammit.

"Do you want to go to the city and check things out?"

I looked up and met Declan's stare. It had iced over, all hint of emotion gone from his expression. "Yes."

"Let's go, then."

I grabbed my daggers, sheathed them at my hips, and slipped my feet into my military-style black leather boots.

I didn't want a fight. But I would be ready if a fight was what we found.

❦

IT TOOK us twenty-two minutes to get to Sanborn Place. Under normal circumstances it took half an hour. I drove the obnoxious orange Hummer Declan insisted on giving me and managed to shave off a few minutes.

It didn't feel like it'd been enough.

Post Street, where Sanborn Place was located, was quiet. The streetlamps were on, illuminating the bare sidewalks.

It was late. But it wasn't *that* late. There should still be cars parked on the streets and people strolling about.

I drove into the lower parking garage and parked.

Declan's expression was grim as we exited the vehicle. There were two other cars parked in the garage. Both sported vinyl stickers on the back windows that read Diamond Rock Construction.

Christian and his crew hadn't left yet. But if that was the case, why wasn't anyone answering their phones?

We climbed the flight of stairs leading to the street entrance.

"It's too quiet."

I nodded.

I scanned the streets for any hint of movement but found nothing. The front door was open.

If was after nine, and our posted office hours said we closed at six. Things should have been locked up for the night by now.

The office was dark. I flicked on the lights, and Declan snarled beside me.

Three bodies lay face down on the carpet.

Shit.

I rushed forward and checked the man on the left. Declan checked the two on the right.

"I have a pulse." I breathed a sigh of relief. He was alive.

"Same with these two."

I rolled the man over and recognized Christian's Hispanic features. I scanned his body for any injuries.

"No blood. Nothing feels broken."

I gave Christian a shake.

He moaned but didn't open his eyes.

Declan situated the other two workers on their backs, made sure they were breathing, and came over to help me.

"Christian? Christian, wake up." I shook him again.

His head lolled to the side, and saliva dripped from the corner of his mouth.

"I don't know what's wrong with him."

Declan lifted his eyelids. "Pupils are blown."

I frowned. "What does that mean?"

"He's drugged." Declan lifted Christian's dead weight and carried him like a baby in his arms as though he weighed nothing.

"I'm going to put him in the car. Watch the other two, and if anyone steps through that door that isn't me, stab them."

I rolled my eyes, but nodded. I could do that.

Declan removed each worker from the room, one after the other. He made quick work of it, and within ten minutes, the office was empty of everyone but us.

"Inarus isn't here."

Inarus was a teleportation capable TK. If he wasn't back at the Compound, why wasn't he here?

Declan crouched beside Inarus' desk and inhaled. "His scent is strongest here." He touched the carpet.

"He ports in on that spot. He doesn't usually use doors unless he has to."

Declan frowned. "His scent trail begins here, but it leaves through the front doors. It's heavy. When a person walks in or out of a room, their scent trail is light. They don't spend a significant amount of time in any one place, so their scent lingers in the air for a short time. Inarus' scent is embedded in the carpet. He was dragged."

I cursed. "We need to get the others to the Compound and hope Frankie can wake them. I want to know what the hell happened."

Declan rose from his crouch. "You and me both."

I shut off the lights and locked the office on our way out.

Movement on our right caught my attention.

"Vampire." Declan spat the word like it was dirty.

I drew both my daggers from my waist.

Two vampires approached but made no overtly threatening movements. When they were fifteen feet away, they stopped and looked each of us up and down like they were surveying an insect under a microscope.

The vampire on my right had rust-colored hair combed back to smooth perfection. Dressed in a three-piece black suit that was clearly tailored, he was the picture-perfect businessman.

The vampire to my left was his complete opposite. He sported ripped denim jeans, a wide-necked, sleeveless shirt, and had shoulder length blue-black hair that framed his hard-edged face.

Of the two, I was more worried about Mr. Suit.

Ripped Jeans smiled in my direction, displaying twin rows of razor-sharp teeth.

Wonderful. Clearly he was one for the dramatics.

"We've been waiting for you," Suit said. His voice was cultured, with a hint of a European accent.

"As you can see, I've arrived. What can I do you for?"

Ripped Jeans took a menacing step forward.

"I wouldn't," I warned.

He ignored me, and with lightning speed, reached for my throat. His hand was a blur, but Declan caught the movement and twisted the vampire's arm behind his back.

Crack.

He howled in pain.

"I did warn you."

Mr. Suit scowled but made no move to help his companion.

Ripped Jeans struggled for a moment, and Declan twisted again. Another bone snapped.

"If I were you, I'd stop moving and state your business."

"Release me at once."

I sent a questioning look to Declan.

Gold flecks filled his gaze. He smiled.

"Sorry. He's having too much fun. Let's try this again. What do you want?"

Mr. Suit answered. "My employer requests an audience."

I kept my eyes on him, trusting Declan to keep Ripped Jeans under control.

"Who's your employer?"

He smiled and shook his head.

So it was going to be like that? Alright, then.

"Tell your employer I respectfully decline. Have a good night."

Declan shoved Ripped Jeans away from him.

His right arm hung limp at his side, and he whirled on us with a snarl but didn't lunge.

I tightened my grip on my daggers.

The idiot wasn't going to walk away.

"That is ..." Suit paused for a moment as though searching for the right word. "Unfortunate."

I braced myself.

Ripped Jeans lunged low, aiming for Declan's knees. He managed to wrap his arms around one leg, but Declan caught him around the waist, hefted him into the air, and threw him across the street like he was throwing a dodgeball.

The other vampire took me in the stomach. With lightning speed, he crashed into me, shoving me off my feet and onto the pavement.

We rolled on the ground, each trying to gain the upper hand.

I plunged one dagger into his side between the fourth and fifth ribs. The blade slid in with little resistance. I twisted the handle and felt my dagger scrape bone.

Mr. Suit snarled and lunged for my throat.

On instinct I shoved my arm up, and instead he got a mouthful of leather.

I pulled my dagger out and stabbed again.

His eyes glowed amber, and I stabbed a third time.

"Get. Off. Of. Me!"

The vampire was jerked aside and thrown into Sanborn Place's brick exterior. I climbed to my feet to see Declan pick him back up before slamming the vampire's body down onto the pavement.

Concrete cracked.

"That wasn't me!" I said as Ripped Jeans suddenly came out of nowhere with a left hook aimed at my face.

I dodged, but not fast enough. Pain bloomed across my face, and a turbulent rage rolled through me.

Fire broke out over my skin. I peeled my leather jacket off and saw horror fill Ripped Jeans's face as flames danced over every inch of my exposed flesh.

I directed my fire behind him, building a wall of flames and boxing him in.

He stared around with a wild look in his eyes. "What the fuck are you?"

"I'm Aria. It's nice to meet you. I have a few questions, and you're going to answer them." I advanced.

He backed away, but there was nowhere for him to go.

"There are several ways a vampire can die. You can rip out their heart. Stab them in the heart with silver. Decapitate them. Or my personal favorite, light them on fire and watch them dissolve into ash. It's pretty gruesome but, effective."

"Honey—" Declan stood and wiped his bloody hands onto his jeans.

Mr. Suit lay unmoving on the ground, his chest ripped open, and his heart lying in the dirt beside him.

"Mmhmm?"

"Just finish him."

I mock scowled. "Are you sure? I had questions. But if you think it'd be better to—"

"I'll answer. Ask away. I'm happy to help."

I turned back to Ripped Jeans with a smile.

He flinched.

Point one to Aria.

"Who's your employer?"

"I don't know. Riggs got the call and payment was deposited into our accounts. We never met the guy."

"Riggs?"

He waved toward his dead friend. Ah, Mr. Suit.

Alright, then. "After you captured us, where were you told to take us?"

"Not both of you. Orders were to sit on the building until a woman matching your description arrived. We were to apprehend you alive, and then call for the drop off point. There was no mention of a guy."

"What happened here before we arrived?"

Ripped Jeans shook his head. "Dunno. It's been quiet the last few hours."

Well, that told me one thing. Whatever happened to Inarus and the rest of the crew happened during daylight hours.

Vampires didn't come out during the day. At least not if they could help it. There was a reason that legend said vampires couldn't go out in the sun, and they were almost right about why.

If a vampire was fewer than five undead years, they could manage direct sun exposure for anywhere from thirty minutes to an hour. Any older than five undead years, and they could only manage a matter of minutes.

It had to do with the lack of water content in a vampire's body after the change. Sun exposure caused severe dehydration at an accelerated rate. Too long, and the vampire would dry out to a husk and shortly after that, their body would decompose and turn to ash.

There was no coming back after that.

Ripped Jeans didn't strike me as newly made, so he wouldn't linger outside until the sun had set.

"Was anyone assigned to look out for me before you arrived?"

He shook his head. "Nah. This was a two-man job. Just me and Riggs."

I considered that.

Declan growled beside me, and Ripped Jeans tried to take another step back before the heat of the flames caused him to jump forward.

"You're not playing bait."

I glared at him. "I—"

"No. There is no way I'm letting you—"

My vision turned red. "You're not *letting* me do anything. I don't need your permission. I'm a grown a—"

"Err ... sorry to interrupt, but can I go now?"

I whirled on Ripped Jeans.

"No!"

"I can see you two could use some privacy. Maybe it would be best if—"

"She said, NO!" Declan roared at the vampire. Actually roared.

I couldn't help the snicker that escaped me.

"What's so damn funny?" Declan asked.

"Absolutely nothing." I turned back to Ripped Jeans. "You're going to help me. We're going to pretend like you're actually good at your job, and you're going to deliver me to the drop."

Declan growled beside me. I ignored it, but it looked like Ripped Jeans was having a hard time with it, so I pulled on my fire and tightened the surrounding walls.

"Okay. Okay. I'll do it."

"Glad we got that settled. Come on, honey, you can lurk in the shadows and be all scary while I play bait."

Chapter Twelve

I f I thought I could send Declan to the Compound with the others while Ripped Jeans and I figured out who wanted me delivered, I would have but even I knew a losing battle when I saw one.

So, we had a cozy car ride from Sanborn Place with three unconscious shifters in the back seat and our new vampire friend wedged between Declan and I in the front.

Declan drove.

I kept an eye on our new friend while playing with a ball of fire the size of a grapefruit the entire way.

Ripped Jeans proved he wasn't a complete idiot.

He sulked in silence, made no threatening gestures, and kept his mouth firmly closed and fangs hidden away.

The level of stillness a vampire could achieve gave me the heebie jeebies. But I was grateful he didn't decide to force our hand by attacking.

We needed this lead.

Brock met us at the Compound gates with a group of men. They carted out our injured with instructions to have the workers taken straight to Annabeth and Frankie and that Declan wanted an update as soon as the Pack Healers knew anything.

Brock lingered beside the driver's-side door and eyed the Vampire seated between us.

"Anything I should know?"

I shook my head. "Nope. We're just having a date night." I smiled.

Declan growled and said something to Brock that I couldn't hear before we pulled away and headed for the drop point.

We'd just made it off Pack land when Declan said, "This is not a date." His tone was gravelly, and dark shadows played across his face.

"Why not? I like these kinds of dates." In a twisted sort of way, I did. This, I could get behind. It was my normal. I didn't do fancy dinners or movies. They were pretentious. If I wanted to get to know someone, I wanted to see them in their element, behaving how they did every single day.

This was my element. Maybe Declan would see me in all my glory and head for the hills.

I eyed him warily. *Probably not.*

The reasonable part of me wished he would. Being with me could only end in misery. I was enough of a mess before, even more so now that dear old Mom was back in the picture.

Declan was a shifter. My mother would always try to crush the Pack. She wanted humans back on top of the food chain, and she didn't care how she got there or who was hurt in the process.

If he were smart, he would leave me.

I really hoped he wasn't smart.

The drop point was located in Airway Heights across from the Maverick gas station just off the highway.

We pulled up to an abandoned warehouse and parked.

"Make the call." I nudged him with my elbow and snuffed out my fire.

Ripped Jeans pulled out his phone and dialed.

"I got the girl… No, he can't talk… Because he's dead, that's why… Alright. Alright. See you in thirty."

He hung up the phone and shoved it in his pocket.

"Well?" I said.

In a very human gesture, he shrugged his shoulders. "Well what?"

"What did they say?"

He glowered at me, and red tinged his irises. "I don't know why you're asking me. Ask him. He heard it all."

I flicked my gaze toward Declan, who nodded.

I glared. "Would someone please explain to the one person without super hearing powers what the hell the bad guys said?"

Ripped Jeans snickered.

"Screw you both. Let's get this show on the road."

WE'D AGREED on the ride over that Declan would find a dark spot to hide in, so he loped off to go make himself invisible.

Ripped Jeans found a rock to sit on and made himself look bored. I didn't think he had to try very hard. I lay in the dirt, feigning unconsciousness.

"Did it have to be in the dirt with all the bugs," I whispered. "There was a nice grassy spot—"

He hissed, "Shut up. Someone's coming."

I clamped my lips shut, closed my eyes, and prayed the vampire didn't screw me over. We'd threatened death and dismemberment, but Ripped Jeans seemed like the type to hold a grudge. Here's to hoping he valued his life more than his pride.

A vehicle rumbled in the distance, growing closer.

Headlights reflected over my body, and I forced myself to remain still.

Someone got out of a car. A door closed. Then another. At least two people approached.

I held my breath.

"I delivered the girl. I want my money."

"Is she alive?"

Was that worry I heard in the man's voice?

"She's alive. Drugged. Now, my money."

Something was thrown, and Ripped Jeans caught it. I heard the distinct sound of a zipper. He was probably looking inside a bag to make sure he got whatever he was promised.

"Nice doing business with you."

Air whooshed around me.

Sonovabitch. He was gone. He'd left, just like that.

I ground my teeth together and waited to see what these two would do.

"Come on. Grab the girl, and let's go before anyone comes by."

Invisible hands lifted my body off the ground.

Shit.

Psykers.

My eyes snapped opened. I tried to move, but my body was held immobile in the air.

My body followed the two men back to a car. I had to break out of this.

I called my fire to me. It responded in a rush of heat through my bloodstream, but nothing else happened.

Shit.

I took a breath. *Come on, Aria. Get it together.*

I didn't know where Declan was, but I knew he wouldn't let these two take off with me. I trusted in that and called on the violent telekinetic power inside of me. The one I did my best to ignore.

I still didn't know how to control it, but today it snapped through me like a lightning strike. The air crackled around me and the two men whirled to stare at my body, still hovering off the ground.

"What the—"

I hammered through their telekinetic hold. One man staggered back, clutching his head as my body crashed to the pavement.

Hurts, doesn't it?

I had firsthand experience with my own telekinetic hold being broken. The backlash was brutal.

I jumped to my feet and pulled my daggers from my sides. Flames rolled across my body and covered my blades.

"Hi."

Both men backed away slowly with their hands raised.

"We don't want any trouble. We just want to talk."

I quirked a brow. "You have a really strange way of showing it. You had me kidnapped. Is that supposed to endear you to me?"

One of the men seemed to gather himself. He took a step forward. "I'm Jason Hoang. This is Emerson Suede." He indicated the man standing beside him. "We don't mean you any harm. We tried to get in touch with you through the proper channels, but we were stonewalled."

I folded my arms over my chest, careful to keep from pricking my jacket with my blades. "And what channels would those be?"

Jason ticked them off one by one. "We attempted your former residence and were told by a Harpy that you had moved to the Compound."

That'd be Melody, my Harpy friend and former neighbor. I really should give her a call and see how she was doing.

"We then tried to call through the Compound's public assistance number. We called eleven times, and each time were told you were unavailable."

Well, there had been a lot going on these past few months.

"We then tried to get ahold of you through Sanborn Place

but were repeatedly told that you were out of the office and then that the office was closed for repairs."

Okay. So maybe these two had done everything in their power to get ahold of me, but that still didn't give them a free pass on having me kidnapped.

"Don't you think hiring vampire thugs to kidnap and drug me was a little overkill?"

Jason frowned. "We gave him no such instructions."

I almost believed him. Jason had that friendly, boy-next-door demeanor that made you want to trust him.

Emerson jumped in. "Look. We hired the vamps to track you down, tell you that you were needed, and convince you to meet us here at all costs while ensuring your safety. We didn't say anything about kidnapping or drugging you."

Well, that was reassuring at least. Assuming what they said was true.

At that moment, Declan decided to come out of the shadows and make himself known.

Both men froze like a deer caught in headlights and eyed Declan's approach with open apprehension.

"Well, now that everyone is here. Why don't we get to the meat and potatoes of it all? What do you two want?"

Chapter Thirteen

"We need protection." Emerson said.

I hadn't paid him as much attention as I had Jason, but now that Declan stood beside me, I gave each of the men a good once over.

Emerson Suede wore ripped jeans and a faded, blue cotton shirt. His shoulder-length, blond hair was pulled back at his nape, making his face more angular. Sharper. But there was something relaxed about his stance.

He didn't seem worried.

And that had me worried.

Jason Hoang was dressed similarly. Ripped jeans and a simple cotton shirt, but his dark, almost black, hair was shaved on both sides, leaving the top longer. He had almond-shaped eyes and a full mouth.

He was of Asian descent but probably mixed with European blood somewhere in his line, since his Asian features were less severe.

Neither man looked threatening. But at least one was a psyker. Likely both of them. I'd be an idiot to let my guard down around either of them.

"And who exactly is it that you're wanting me to protect you from?" If this was a gig, then they should have gone through Sanborn Place. Clients didn't get to pick which merc took on the gig. They submitted the job, and someone was assigned. Granted, now we were down to just Inarus and I, but the system was still the same. And lately Inarus had been the one taking the bulk of the case load.

"Viola Reynolds."

But that one name had my attention.

Emerson shifted from foot to foot. "Look. Can we go inside? It's not safe standing out in the open like this."

I didn't like the idea of going anywhere with the two of them, but if they really were hiding from my mother, or the HAC for that matter, I'd be antsy standing out in the open too.

I nodded, and Declan and I followed them toward the building.

Every one of my senses was on high alert, and I still hadn't called my fire back, but I did sheathe both my blades.

Jason was a telekinetic. That'd been easy enough to figure out, since the blowback from breaking his telekinetic hold had left him staggering.

I wondered what Emerson was, though.

Once inside, my eyes tried to adjust to the dark.

Jason flipped a switch on the wall, illuminating the large room.

Workbenches were scattered throughout the room. Rusted old tools and dirt-coated debris littered the floor. This was probably an old metal foundry from the looks of it.

I walked over to one of the tables, Declan at my side, and jumped up to sit on its surface. A fine layer of grime stained my palms where I'd touched the table.

I wiped it on my jeans and managed to leave a dark streak along my thigh. Wonderful.

Declan leaned against the table beside me. Agitation radiated from him and through our bond.

I rolled my neck and tried to push his emotions out of me.

Jason and Emerson leaned against a table across from us, both careful not to touch the grime-covered surface.

"So why do you need protection from Viola?" We might as well dive right in.

Declan's shoulder brushed against me. I pulled my fire back. It wouldn't help my position if I burned my back up.

"We see the writing on the wall, and we don't like where things are going for our people."

I drummed my fingers along the table's smooth surface and made a smiley face in the gunk. "Who are your people, exactly?" Psykers weren't organized. We weren't like a Shifter Pack or a Vampire Seethe. We were loners. We blended in seamlessly with humanity, so there had never been any reason to separate ourselves. We also had no way to distinguish each other from the crowd without a blatant use of power.

"PsyShade needs a way out."

My eyebrows rose. "PsyShade, as in the elite group of assassins who work for the HAC? Is that the PsyShade you're referring to here? Because last I heard, you all were sitting pretty comfortably as underlings for the HAC. Why do you all of a sudden want out now?"

"It's complicated."

Oh, I bet it is. I laughed. A full-on belly laugh that had me leaning forward in hysterics.

"You mean to—" I couldn't get the words out. I laughed harder.

"Aria?" Declan's voice was hesitant.

I snorted. "This is so rich." I wiped tears from my eyes. "You want my help?"

"We do," Jason answered. "We don't have a lot of options. If we did, we wouldn't have gone to such lengths to secure a meeting with you."

I snorted. "PsyShade is the same group of assholes that attacked my friend." They'd hunted Inarus mercilessly. I'd found him beaten and bloodied in my apartment when he ran out of places to go to get away from them. He'd been one of their own, and they'd still hunted him down like a dog. "PsyShade attacked me. Destroyed my place of work. Why would I help you?"

They had to be delusional. They were my enemies. I didn't care how much they paid, this was a gig I had every intention of turning down.

"We're willing to pay for your servi—"

I held my hand up, stopping Jason before he finished his sentence. "There isn't enough money in the world." I shook my head and leaned back on my hands. "What reason do I have to help you? Give me one reason, and I'll take it under consideration. But from where I'm sitting, you're the enemy."

Jason pursed his lips together, forming a thin white line. "We don't have to be your enemy. We can be allies. You could use our strength and support as much as we can use yours. This can be a mutually beneficial arrangement."

Before I could reject his statement, Declan reached out and twined his fingers with mine. I looked down and stared at our joined hands and then up at him. "They could be a means for stopping your mother," Declan said.

I scowled. "And if they turn on us? They've been a part of the HAC for who knows how long. What's to say they don't harbor the same beliefs? That shifters, vampires, witches, and every other paranormal in existence is beneath them and in need of exterminating?"

Declan shrugged his shoulders. "Ask them."

It wasn't that easy though. Was it?

I leveled my gaze on the two men in front of me. "I'm not alone. I'm mated to Declan." I lifted our joined hands. "Aligning yourselves with me would mean aligning yourselves with the Pack."

Neither man made any indication that they objected to that fact.

"Okay, with that settled, I want to clear the air." I waited for them both to nod before I continued. "I don't trust you. I have no way of knowing this isn't a set up. But if you're honest and forthcoming with information, I'll consider helping you. And if you lie to me or try to harm anyone I care about, I'll kill both of you and won't think twice about it. Are we clear?"

"Crystal." Jason said. "Let us bring you up to speed."

"The HAC started recruiting Psykers five years ago. We were scattered for the most part, but they gave us safety and a place to call home." Emerson paused.

Safety after the Awakening was hard to come by. I'd been on my own at the age of seventeen just six months after the Awakening. Had someone offered me safety, food, shelter, and the comforts of home, I probably would have taken them up on it. But by the time anyone had come looking for me, I'd already been on the streets and worked my way out of them. And I'd learned that help always came with a price.

"They weren't so fanatical back then. The HAC was an authority that promised to restore the life we all grew up having. I was twenty-one at the time. I'd watched friends die at the hands of vampires. So I took their offer and never looked back. Until now."

"What's changed?"

Some silent communication passed between both men before Emerson continued. "We might not have been there when you were brought in. But we know what was done to you. We know that Viola ordered Aiden to pull out your pyrokinetic power, and we know that you killed him for it."

Declan growled deep in his chest.

Emerson raised both his hands. "We don't blame you. Aiden deserved what he got."

Declan's growl quieted, but it didn't lessen the feel of his anger through the bond.

"And why does that matter to you?"

Jason took one step forward. "I'm a TK, like Aiden was. Emerson is an aerokinetic."

That was great, but where were they going with this?

"Viola is separating non-TKs from PsyShade. We didn't realize it for what it was in the beginning. But over the past few months, she's been thinning the herd. TKs are the most universal power. A geokinetic requires earth. An aerokinetic needs air. All the other designations need an element to use their powers. We don't. She's been separating us from the others little by little and molding us to think we're better. She's brainwashing our fucking people, and most don't even realize it." Jason's breathing was heavy as if he'd just run a marathon. Anger marked his face, and small particles of dust danced around his legs.

He was struggling to keep his abilities in check.

Glad to see I wasn't the only one with this problem.

"She pulled all the TKs aside last week. Every one of us. She wants us to purge the others."

I sucked in a sharp breath as horror washed over me. The feel of my pyrokinetic abilities being ripped from inside of me was unlike any pain I'd experienced before. I wouldn't wish it on anyone.

"I kept my mouth shut. I didn't want to rebel out in the open. Viola isn't known for tolerating disobedience." Jason looked down at his feet.

My stomach clenched, a pit already forming. "What happened?"

"Seven of our men were murdered over the next couple of days. No one knows exactly how, but each one went out on an assignment, and their dead bodies came back. We all know she ordered the hits, but we don't know who executed them. She's looked outside of our ranks for assassins before. But she may have also convinced one of our own to take them out." He shrugged. "I won't purge my own people. And I won't let myself be killed and abandon them either. I need a way to get them out. Fast."

I looked at Declan, indecision warring inside of me.

"So far they've spoken nothing but the truth," Declan said.

I chewed my lower lip. I had to take on my mother either way. If she was purging her ranks, all that did was help me. But if her ranks became mine …

"How many psykers are there?"

"Fifty-two," Emerson said.

I whistled. That was a lot of psychokinetic power.

"There is one problem."

Only one? I quirked a brow and waited for him to continue.

"We don't know who we can trust. Those who initially spoke out are already dead. And the others aren't stupid enough to speak out now."

"So then what's your plan? Please tell me you didn't go to all this trouble"—I waved at the empty space around me —"to get me here only to leave me hanging? Because I can't really help you, assuming I even want to, if you don't know what people you want to pull out of there."

Jason interjected, "We intend to start with the non TKs. That's thirty-four men and women. After we secure them, we can figure out how to approach the remaining eighteen."

"I still don't see what you want from me. What exactly are you expecting me to do?"

"We don't need you to do anything. Not at first. We can get our people out. But we have nowhere to go. All of our money is tied up in HAC-owned accounts. Any large withdrawals would draw suspicion. We need—"

"A Compound," I finished for him.

I turned to Declan. They hadn't tracked me down because I

could do anything for them. They'd tracked me down because of my connection to Declan and the built-in security the Compound provided. They needed Pack protection. But I didn't speak for the Pack, and their protection wasn't mine to give.

A cell phone buzzed in the silence. Declan ignored the silent question that hung in the air and read the text that illuminated his screen.

"Christian is awake. We need to return and see what happened to …" He trailed off.

Shit. Inarus.

I turned back to Emerson and Jason. "You're asking a lot."

"We know," Jason said.

"We won't be able to give you an answer tonight."

Both men nodded. "We figured as much."

I chewed my lower lip and sent a furtive glance towards Declan. *To tell them, or not to tell them?*

"Inarus is missing," Declan said.

Well, I guess that took care of it.

Startled eyes met my gaze. But before I could say anything, Declan continued, "He was taken from Sanborn Place earlier today. Help us find him, and you'll have your answers."

"Consider it done."

Jason reached out and wrapped a hand around Emerson's wrist, and they were gone.

Chapter Fourteen

Christian was awake and eating when we walked into his room. Still pale and visibly shaken, it was a relief when Annabeth told us he wouldn't suffer any permanent damage from the attack.

"The drugs are still wearing off. Be patient with him, alright?" Annabeth said.

I nodded and took a seat in a nearby armchair.

Declan stood beside the bed, eyes downcast as he surveyed Christian for injuries. "Annabeth says you had a concussion."

It wasn't a question, but Christian nodded anyway. "It's healed. I fell over like the freaking Leaning Tower of Pisa. My limbs locked up. I couldn't stop my fall."

I winced. That had to hurt.

"What happened?"

It was the million-dollar question. How does someone get inside my office and incapacitate three full-grown shifters and a telekinetic without leaving any trace of who or what they were?

"They gassed us. One minute I was working as usual, and the next my head started spinning and the ground rushed up to meet my face."

"Did you see anyone?"

Christian shook his head.

Damn.

"Think," Declan growled. "Sounds. Scents. Anything."

A furrow formed between Christian's brows. "Three sets of boots. Heavy. Human scent, but unfamiliar. No one I've come across before." He shook his head. "I'm sorry. That's all I've got."

Declan placed an arm on his shoulder. "It'll have to do. Get some rest. If anything else comes to mind, call me."

Christian nodded, and we left the room, giving him time to recuperate.

Declan didn't say anything until we made our way to his room. He kicked off his boots and took a seat in one of the lounge chairs facing the fireplace while I paced behind him.

"Come sit down."

I shook my head. I couldn't sit. I needed to think.

Declan captured my wrist and tugged me toward him, pulling me into his lap. He kissed me. A gentle press of his lips before leaning his forehead against mine. "It's something."

It wasn't. We were right where we'd started. With Inarus missing and no idea who'd taken him. "He's one of mine." He was one of my people. I was responsible for him. I didn't have many people in my life I cared about or who cared about me. I had to find him.

Declan tucked a strand of hair behind my ear. "I know."

He didn't seem happy with the admission.

I sighed and curled into him, tucking my head beneath his chin.

"We know whoever attacked him was human. That's something."

He was right. But it wasn't entirely helpful. There were two hundred and twelve thousand humans in Spokane. Finding the ones responsible for this would be like finding a needle in a haystack.

I worried my lower lip.

A knock at the door had me sitting up. I moved to climb out of Declan's lap but his firm grip on my hips held me immobile.

"Come in," he said.

The door opened, and Robert stepped inside.

He grinned when he caught sight of the two of us. "Glad to see my favorite couple is doing well."

After what Derek had told me earlier, I wasn't so sure about that, but I chose to ignore my doubts. Robert had done nothing to show me he couldn't be trusted. Until he did … I would leave things alone and take his words at face value.

"What do you need?" Declan's tone was brisk, and I didn't miss the flash of irritation that crossed Robert's face.

"Dia wishes to see her brother. Do you know when he'll be returning?"

Well, crap. We were going to have to tell her.

"No."

Robert frowned. "No, she can't see him? Or No, you don't know when he'll be returning?" A crease formed between his brows.

"Inarus is missing," I said. There was no point in hiding it.

"Do you intend to find him?" The question was directed at Declan, but I answered it.

"Of course, we will."

Robert's gaze stayed locked on Declan, still waiting for a response.

Declan nodded.

"I'll let our guest know. She'll want to be involved in the search."

I cursed under my breath.

"What was that?"

"Nothing," I gritted out. Of course she'd want to be involved. And I should want her to be. The more hands on deck the better.

But having Dia involved meant I had to work with her. And I needed to do it without killing her.

Easier said than done.

"Relevant details?"

"He was abducted at Sanborn Place. Three men. They gassed out the building, knocked out the construction crew, and grabbed only Inarus. Christian said their attackers were human. That's all he could discern before he blacked out."

Robert nodded. "I'll bring Brock up to speed if you haven't already and find a delicate way to break the news to Dia. You'll keep me apprised of any updates?"

Declan nodded, and Robert left.

"Why is he so interested?" Robert didn't like Inarus, and from what he'd told us, he was only playing Dia. So why did any of this matter to him?

"He's scheming. The more information he has, the more he can manipulate. Don't bother trying to figure Robert out. I gave up years ago, and it's the only reason I've managed to maintain my sanity."

I snorted. "Fine. But only because he might be able to help." I leaned back down against Declan's chest and watched the logs in the fireplace crackle. Inarus' disappearance ate at me. Why would anyone take him? The only enemy I could think of would be the HAC. But why now? And why him?

The door burst open, and I jumped from Declan's lap.

He stood at the same time, and thankfully I hadn't tumbled to the ground.

Dia stood in the doorway, her blue-gray eyes wild. "Where's my brother?" she snarled.

Well, that didn't take long.

Robert strode in right behind her. "She didn't take the news well."

Dia sneered at him. "Of course I didn't take the news well.

My brother is missing, and you two are in here canoodling while he's God knows where."

I glared daggers at her. "We've been back for all of ten minutes. I'm not just sitting on my hands, okay? But we don't have anything to go on right now. What do you want me to do, knock on every door and pass out a missing person poster?"

"Yes! If that's what it takes." Dia shook her wrist at us. "Take this off. Get this stupid thing off of me, and I'll find him myself."

That would have been a great idea. If only it were that easy.

"I can't."

"You can't, or you won't?"

"Can't," I said through clenched teeth. Though even if I could, I wasn't entirely sure I would. I didn't trust Dia as far as I could throw her. For all I knew, she was somehow involved in Inarus' disappearance, and this was just a ploy for her freedom.

"Why the hell not?" Dia stalked forward and got in my face. "Do you even want my brother to be found?"

I shoved her away from me, a snarl on my lips. "Of course I want him found! But the magic doesn't work that way. You're bound for two weeks. There's nothing we can do about it. It will fall off on its own when the spell has expired. Until then, you're bound. Deal with it."

Fury washed over her face. Had her powers been free, I was certain the entire Compound would be shaking right now.

The hairs on my arms stood on end.

"If anything happens to him—"

"I'm going to get him back."

"How? What do you have? From what Robert said, you have nothing." She threw her hands in the air and stalked away from me.

I shot Robert a glare.

He shrugged as if to say, *Well, you don't.*

Asshat.

"You're right. We don't have much. All we know is the

building was gassed and three men came in and took him out the front door while the rest of the crew on site was unconscious."

Dia froze, her eyes narrowed, and a crease formed between her brows. "Was Inarus unconscious when he was taken?"

We didn't have any way to be sure, but Declan had been confident that Inarus had put up a fight. "We don't think so."

Declan interjected. "The scent trail was too heavy. There was a struggle."

"The HAC has him."

"How can you know?" I often blamed my mother. It always seemed like the right thing to do since she was usually the evildoer involved. But I had no evidence pointing in her direction on this one.

"The gas. The HAC formulated a special gas. It dampens our abilities."

"How?"

"It plays with your brain chemistry. If you're a psyker, it makes it difficult for you to send commands from your brain through your body to access your abilities. If you're a non-psyker, it puts you to sleep. I don't know how long it would keep a non-psyker down, but it only incapacitates us for a matter of minutes. That's why they came in with multiple bodies. Three against one. If Inarus is anything like he was growing up, he relies entirely on his abilities. He doesn't carry weapons. They probably did. Three armed men would be enough to subdue him long enough to inject him with an actual sedative."

I swore. "How confident are you that the HAC is involved?" Given their past history and previous attempts on Inarus' life, they were the only ones I could think of who'd want him, but what didn't add up for me was the abduction.

Before, the HAC had tried to kill Inarus on site to prevent him from spilling any of their secrets. But it'd been weeks since the last attack. Why strike again when whatever Inarus knew had already been shared, and why abduct him when they could have just killed him while the others were knocked out?

"Almost positive."

I paced the small space in front of me. "I don't know where they would have taken him. Do you?"

Dia shook her head. We weren't getting anywhere.

"I don't work on this side of the country. I'm an east coast recruit only recently arrived because I requested the transfer. I don't know all their hidey holes for this area, assuming they kept him local."

They would. My mother wouldn't have Inarus abducted unless she intended to hold him over me. Was that why he'd been taken?

"We need to get in touch with Jason and Emerson."

"Who?" Dia asked.

I brought her up to speed on our activities of the day.

She whistled. "Your mother is a real piece of work."

I rolled my eyes. "I'm aware." I scratched the back of my neck. "I'll try and get ahold of the guys. See if they've found anything or if they have any idea of where we can start looking."

"Let me go back in."

I frowned. "What?"

"Let me go. I'll go back to my checkpoint and see what I can find out from the inside."

I shook my head. "That's a horrible idea. It's been over a week since the attack. They'll wonder where you've been. You'll get yourself killed."

Dia shook her head vehemently. "I have to do something. I can't just sit here while my brother is missing. Let me do this. Please. I'll come up with a story about being taken, sedated, and escaping when I finally came to."

I didn't like it. Dia's wellbeing wasn't my concern, but if she wound up killed, Inarus would never forgive me.

Robert stepped forward. "I'll cover her. I can't go in with her, but I can remain close and in communication. I'll have two more of Clan Cadinae on site as well should we need back up or should we need to extricate Dia."

I turned to Declan, wondering what he thought of this. "She could give him up the moment she walks inside."

"Hey! I wouldn't do that!" Dia exclaimed.

Declan shrugged. "We don't know you," he said and turned back to Robert. "But I trust your judgment. If you think sending her in has merit, then go. See Brock before you leave, and he'll get you set up with communications."

"Thank you." Robert said and turned to leave.

"Dia," Declan called. She stopped in the doorway and turned to face him. "If my men don't come back, I'll hold you responsible."

She swallowed hard, but nodded and left the room.

Chapter Fifteen

The bed dipped, and a warm body slid in beside me.

Warm hands splayed across my bare stomach, pulling me tight against an equally bare and muscled chest. The smell of pine and mint filled my nose, and I snuggled deeper into the embrace.

Declan nuzzled my shoulder, his five o'clock shadow rough against my skin, causing goosebumps to break out along my flesh.

"Why do you insist on sleeping in here?" he asked.

I sighed and pulled the covers up higher toward my face. Sun filtered in through the window, letting me know it was morning, but I still wasn't ready to get up.

"It's my bedroom," I mumbled. "Where else would I sleep?"

A growl vibrated through his chest and along my back. "This is a guest room. Your place is with me. In *our* room."

A ghost of a smile tilted the corners of my mouth. I knew it bothered him that I hadn't moved into his room but *come on*. I'd just accepted this whole mate bond thing a little over a week ago. Living in the Compound was a pretty big step if you asked me. And living in his quarters was an even bigger step. And while the idea of waking up beside him every morning had its appeal, I wanted to give us time to get to know one another, and if I was being honest with myself, I sometimes needed my own space. A room to escape to when he was driving me up the wall. Not that I would tell him that.

"It's only been a week," I mumbled. Sleep still tinged my voice, and I yawned.

"A week is plenty long enough," he said. "I want you by my side. I want to fall asleep beside you and have you be the first thing I see every morning. I know you're it for me. You feel the same. I know you do. Stop being stubborn and move your things to our room."

Aww, wasn't that sweet?

I rolled over to face him.

"A week is not that long. Most people date for, oh I don't know, a year or more before they move in together."

Declan's lip curled. "I'm not a human. I don't need time to confirm that you're my mate."

I sighed and rolled my eyes. "I know that. But I'm not a shifter. I need time." I reached out and cupped his cheek, brushing my fingers over the stubble on his jaw. "I've accepted the bond. You're my mate. I know that and I ..." My voice trailed off.

I wanted to tell him I loved him. Because I did. With every fiber of my being, I loved him. But the words lodged themselves in my throat.

I swallowed and met his emerald gaze. "I'm still adjusting. If we have forever together, is giving me a little time to adjust too much to ask?"

Declan's lips pressed into a thin line before he leaned down and pressed his lips against mine. "I'll give you time because you want it. But I won't be happy about it. I'm empty when you're not with me."

I melted into a puddle of goo.

Wrapping my arms around his neck, I pulled Declan into a tight embrace and crushed my lips against his, kissing him with a fever I couldn't contain.

He growled and rolled until he was braced on top of me. Looming over me, his eyes filled with gold, his tiger present. "Careful, Aria," he warned.

Careful? I didn't want to be careful. Not with him.

I reached up and tugged him down as I wrapped my legs around his hips. His erection pressed against my abdomen, and I moaned into his mouth.

"Why are you wearing clothes?" I groaned.

Declan chuckled and used one hand to free himself from his boxer briefs. "You're not bare either," he reminded me.

With a quick tug of my panties I remedied that and then unclasped my bra and chucked it over the side of the bed.

"There. Better?"

His chest pressed down against me, and he captured my lips with his. "Much better."

I groaned into his kiss as Declan positioned himself at my entrance. I ground my hips against him, aching for him inside of me.

But he held back, trailing hot, wet kisses down my neck, moving lower until he captured my breast in the wet heat of his mouth.

My back arched off the bed, and I moaned.

I tangled my fingers in the short, white-blonde strands of his hair. "More. God, please, don't stop."

Declan switched to lave my other breast with his attentions, and my insides turned liquid. My breaths came out heavy as fire coursed through my veins. I sucked in a ragged breath and forced myself to calm down. The bed shook, but I ignored it. Nothing was on fire, and the building was still structurally sound. A little bed shaking would be fine.

Pulling Declan up, I kissed him again, and he slid his length deep inside me in one long, powerful thrust.

I cried out while tugging him closer, thrusting my hips up to meet his. My core tightened around him as Declan moved in a chaotic rhythm. Both of us too far gone to care if it was perfect.

God, it felt so damn good.

I moaned into his kiss. Our tongues lashed with one another, and our teeth crashed once or twice with our frenzied movements.

I didn't care. I didn't need perfect. I needed real, and this was it. It was hot and frenzied and everything I craved.

When Declan leaned back to stare down at me, I took advantage and switched our positions. He could have stopped me, but Declan rolled to his back as I pushed his shoulders and settled myself on top of him, straddling his waist without ever breaking contact.

I rocked back and forth on his length. Satisfaction bloomed inside of me with each grunt and groan he made.

His fingers clenched my hips in a bruising grip, and I reveled in the moment as my climax grew closer and closer.

Declan's thumb worked in slow circles over my clit, and I exploded, rocking my hips and crying out as his own climax erupted from him with a roar.

I collapsed on top of him in a sweaty heap. My breaths coming out in labored gasps.

Kissing his neck, I slid off to lie beside him. His chest rose and fell in a steady rhythm, and his emerald eyes shone with barely restrained passion.

He pulled me closer.

"Oh, no. Round two is beyond me right now," I said and tried to wiggle away.

"I think I can make you reconsider."

And he did. With painstaking tenderness he loved me with his body, pushing me to a second climax that left me shaken to my core.

Chapter Sixteen

Robert checked in with Declan twice a day, but he'd had no word from Dia in the three days since she'd walked inside one of the HAC's Spokane facilities.

Worry churned my gut, but Robert seemed positive.

Activity remained low at the HAC site, which he interpreted to mean business was going as usual. If that changed, he'd let us know. Until then, we had to wait.

I sucked at waiting.

On the fourth day, I got a phone call from a phone number I didn't recognize.

"Naveed."

"We found out where Inarus is. He's being held in Sandpoint, Idaho. I can give you the address, but ..." Emerson Suede trailed off.

"But what?" My skin vibrated with anticipation. This was good. We had news. And if the HAC was still holding Inarus, then it meant he was alive.

Relief surged through me at the realization that I wouldn't have to bury my friend.

A sigh on the other line had me holding my breath. "But I don't know how you could possibly get him out without starting a full scale war. The Sandpoint facility isn't some hideout. It's a full-fledged encampment with over three hundred men at the ready. It's the HAC's version of a fortress, and it's damn near impregnable."

I sat down. Alone in my room, I stared out the lone window toward the edge of the Compound property and into the sprawling forest. "I won't leave him to rot," I ground out.

"I'm not telling you to. But you need to know what you'd be walking into."

I listened as Emerson told me about the multiple layers of security. The cameras, sensors, and perimeter that was manned by veteran soldiers and psykers alike.

"It won't be easy, and if you go in full bore, you'll get hit with casualties."

"Can he be ported out?" I wasn't a teleport capable telekinetic. At least not that I was aware of. My TK abilities were still too new for me to know for certain. Aiden had been teleport capable, but that didn't necessarily mean the skill had been passed on to me. But if Inarus could be ported out, then dammit, I'd try.

"No. The facility is warded. Our abilities work, but they're dampened. No telekinetic I know of can execute a port in that environment."

There went that idea.

I worried my lower lip. There had to be a way to get him out of there without starting a war. I'd battle for Inarus' life, but I couldn't put Declan and the Pack in the position of doing so. Not when I couldn't guarantee every shifter would make it out alive.

"What would you suggest?" I asked, hoping that he hadn't called with nothing but bad news.

"Call your mother."

My breath hitched, and I pulled the phone away to look at it for a second before returning it to my ear. "What did you just say? Clearly, I must have misheard."

"You didn't. Your best bet is to call her. Viola is behaving erratically. Your call would throw her off balance, and you might be able to convince her to negotiate Inarus' life for yours. I don't expect you to give yourself up, but getting Inarus out of that building will greatly increase your chances of a rescue."

I mulled that over. He had a point.

"Thank you," I told him when it seemed there was nothing left to say.

"Don't thank me. I did it for selfish reasons. Your man said if we helped find him …"

I nodded, and then remembered he couldn't see me. "I remember. I'll let Declan know. You'll need to decide when you want to get the psyker extraction moving and how much support you'll need from the Pack. But Declan is a man of his word."

"We'll talk soon, then."

And with that, he hung up.

I stared down at my phone for several long minutes. Indecision warred within me. Hearing my mother's voice was the last thing I wanted. Each time I did, it split me in two as my mind rebelled between the knowledge that this was the woman who loved me, raised me from birth to my teenage years, and held me tight whenever I cried, yet was also the same woman who'd abandoned me and considered me an abomination she'd rather be rid of.

The child inside of me wanted her mother's acceptance. But the woman knew she'd never have it.

Before I could make up my mind, the door opened and Declan strode inside. I stared up at him, stark pain etched into my soul. Declan sank to his knees in front of me and clasped my hands between his large calloused ones.

"What is it?" He pressed a kiss to my forehead before leveling his concerned gaze on me. "I felt your heart break right here." He placed a palm over his chest. "What has you feeling so broken?"

A single tear slipped out to spill down my cheek. Declan was quick to thumb it away.

I hid my face as pain and rage and an ache so deep I didn't know how to make it go away threatened to consume me.

"Hey. Shh ... Whatever it is. We'll handle it. Together."

I nodded and tried to get my emotions under control. They had to have been going haywire for Declan to have noticed so quickly that he'd rushed to my side.

Taking several deep breaths, I let my cheek sink into his palm as he pulled me close. "I have to call my mother."

Declan stiffened but waited for me to continue.

"Emerson confirmed that she has Inarus. He's in Sandpoint."

He pulled back and tucked a stray strand of hair behind my ear. "Then we go get him."

I was shaking my head before he'd even finished. "This isn't a hideout with a handful of guards. Emerson says they number over three hundred. We can't—I can't ask the Pack to get involved in this. Not when there's another way."

Declan scowled, a furrow forming between twin, white-blond brows. "We go in with a stealth team. Fewer bodies will make it easier to get in and out unseen."

I shook my head again, love rising to clog my throat. How amazing was this man that he would take such risks for me? For someone I knew he loathed, all because that same someone mattered to me.

"Emerson gave me the layout of their security. It won't work. We need Inarus out of that building if we're going to have any chance of rescuing him. And for that to happen, the HAC has to move him. I don't have a choice. I have to call my mother."

THE PHONE SHOOK in my hands as I waited for her to pick up. It'd been weeks since we last spoke, but it felt like years.

As the dial tone continued to ring, I worried that she might have changed her number. What if she did? How would I get ahold of her then? A knot formed in the pit of my stomach.

Just as I was about to hang up, there was a click on the other line, and I held my breath.

"What?" Annoyance filled my mother's voice.

"Hello, Mother," I said into the receiver. Taking a seat across from Declan, I waited to see how she'd react to my call.

It didn't take long for her to compose herself, and all hints of irritation were erased. "Aria, darling. It's wonderful to hear from you. To what do I owe the pleasure?"

I rolled my eyes. As if she didn't know. "Inarus is missing," I told her.

"Oh, my. That's terrible. But why would you be calling me? You know he and I aren't on the best of terms since ... well ... you know."

I sighed. I didn't want to play games. I didn't have the energy for it, but with my mother, it was always a game. "Mother, I know you have him. I'd like him back, please." That last word took considerable effort to force past my lips.

She laughed, and the sound grated along my nerves. "My dear, so what if I do? If I took him, clearly I have a use for him."

Declan squeezed my hand, and I squeezed it back. "You don't need him. You have plenty more telekinetics in your ranks. Why take him?"

She heaved a long-suffering sigh as though I were some petulant child she didn't think she needed to explain herself to. "Inarus is a top level telekinetic. Yes, I have others, but none as powerful as he is. I wouldn't have needed him if you hadn't killed Aiden ..." She let her words trail off.

Fury washed through me. *So what, this was my fault? I should have just let Aiden rip my pyrokinetic abilities from me?*

Flames licked my arms and ran down to my fingertips, forcing me to pull away from Declan's grasp.

No. She was not going to turn this around on me.

"Aiden's death is on your hands, not mine. You never should have done what you did to me. I'm your daughter, for Chrissakes, does that mean nothing to you anymore?"

I didn't want her to answer. She'd either confirm that she didn't care about me anymore, or she'd lie through her teeth and pretend that she still did. Either way I'd still feel like shit, because dammit she was my mother. It shouldn't be too much to ask for some unconditional love here.

"You've turned your back on your own kind and allied yourself with animals." Her words were filled with disgust. "You should be thanking me. I tried to save you."

"You tried to kill me!"

"Think what you'd like, Aria. But the fact remains, you have nothing to offer me in exchange for Inarus, and until you see that you've taken the wrong path, we have nothing left to discuss."

"Wait!" I said before she had the chance to hang up. I knew I'd need to make a deal with the devil. But it didn't make it any easier. "Release him and take me instead."

"I have no need for a rebellious, pyrokinetic daughter."

"What about a telekinetic one?" I asked.

She sucked in a breath. I didn't think she knew that when Aiden tried to take my abilities I'd taken his instead. Her reaction confirmed it.

"Ripping out someone's abilities can go both ways," I told her. "And I took everything Aiden had. I'm as powerful in my TK abilities as he was." Well, that wasn't entirely true, but she didn't need to know that.

I'd taken everything Aiden had, but I still had no idea how to use it.

"You'll come willingly?" she asked, her tone full of suspicion.

"So long as you release Inarus."
"You have a deal."

Chapter Seventeen

We'd agreed to meet at the abandoned Twin Falls temple. She agreed to bring Inarus, and I agreed to come alone.

Declan wasn't happy about it, but there'd been no budging her. Still, I wasn't an idiot, so I wasn't actually going in alone. We'd just make it look that way.

Declan, Brock, and Derek would be my backup should anything go wrong. They planned to arrive an hour before me, find a good hidey-hole to stay in, and then wait for the show to begin.

My mother wanted me. Not as her daughter, but because I was different, and she probably wanted to experiment on me. Again.

And while I'd agreed to trade myself for Inarus' freedom, I'd avoid doing so if I could help it. She didn't play fair, so there was nothing in the rule book that said I had to.

Though we only had three hours, we came up with a rough plan. Locate Inarus, spring an attack, and take off with him without any casualties on our end.

The meeting was supposed to take place three hours after we'd gotten off the phone. With Sandpoint being a two-hour drive, the guys had to take off almost immediately. They'd have time to strategize together on the way, but I'd be stuck trusting they would sort something out.

Declan messaged me once they arrived, letting me know they were in position. We'd decided to refrain from any contact after that to prevent distractions.

Pulling up to the temple, I realized just how empty the surrounding area was. Hell, all it needed was a few tumbleweeds rolling through the empty streets to complete the picture.

I parked the obnoxious orange Hummer and stepped out into the open. My phone buzzed in my back pocket, and I scowled. I thought …

I flipped open the screen and read the message displayed there.

Olivia: The telekinetic has to die.

I didn't bother responding. "The telekinetic" could mean anyone. Inarus, Dia, Jason…hell, even me. I wasn't going to let this get in my head. I had one objective for today: Save Inarus.

Any looming visions would have to wait for another day, because no one was dying during this rescue mission.

Shoving the phone back in my pocket, I surveyed my surroundings. The street was eerily quiet. I shut my door, checked that I had both my blades, and headed for the entrance. We'd agreed to meet on the rooftop. I wasn't sure why she'd picked that spot, but the roof of the temple it was.

I made my way up the thirteen flights of stairs, pausing briefly on the eleventh floor to catch my breath.

Fuck. My old apartment stairs had nothing on this building.

After giving myself a few moments, I climbed higher until I reached the roof access doorway.

I stepped outside.

The rooftop was empty, but since the Twin Falls temple was the tallest standing building in Sandpoint, Idaho at one hundred and fifty-nine feet, I had a clear view of the rest of the buildings, and easily spotted my mother one block over on the rooftop of an adjacent warehouse.

"What the hell?"

A radio crackled to my right, and I stepped forward to pick it up off the lone piece of furniture on the roof—a rusted metal folded chair.

"What kind of game is this?" I called into the radio.

It crackled a few times before my mother's voice came through, loud and clear.

"Aria, my dear." There was a sigh. "It breaks my heart to have to do this, but some lessons must be learned, and this is one you'll have to go through the hard way. No mother wants to see her child go down the wrong path. I hope this consequence will help you adjust your course."

I stared down at the radio before meeting her gaze across the rooftops. *What the hell was she going on about?*

Before I could ask, two men dressed in black fatigues rushed to the front entrance of the temple. With two-by-fours they sealed the front door shut.

My eyes widened, and I rushed to the opposite end of the building to see two more do the same thing to the rear entrance.

"What the hell are you doing?" I gritted through clenched teeth.

I walked back toward the front of the building and lifted the radio to my mouth. "We had a deal."

"We did. But I've changed my mind. Your punishment for your recent behavior will be to stand witness."

She signaled to someone behind her, and I watched in horror as Inarus was dragged from the rooftop access stairway and dropped at my mother's side. He fell in an unmoving heap beside her.

"What are you doing?" I shouted.

She set her radio down and didn't answer.

"Answer me, dammit. What are you doing to him?"

No response.

I screamed in frustration and threw my radio across the street. It crashed into the side of the building she stood on and shattered.

She shook her head as though disappointed.

"This is your last chance, Aria. Join me," she shouted out to me and held out a hand as though I could reach her.

I fisted my hands at my sides and shook my head. "Let him go. That was the deal. Let him go, and I'll come with you."

"It's too late for that. I've tried to be reasonable. I've given you every opportunity to make the right decision."

The right decision? She was delusional.

"You had me kidnapped. You tried to rip my psyker powers out of me. How is going anywhere with you the right decision where my life is concerned?"

"You should be thanking me. Look how strong you've become."

Right. I was stronger. But not because of her. I was stronger because I trained. I practiced. And when that sonovabitch Aiden tried to rip my pyrokinesis out of me, I ripped his telekinesis out of him instead.

I sneered. "Let him go."

"Come with me. Together we can set back World Order. Claim your rightful place by my side. No one else has to suffer. Despite your abilities, you are still human. You can be on the winning side of this."

Every ounce of psyker energy in my body came to attention. What was she playing at? She didn't want me. She never had.

"Last chance. Join me and I will spare the lives of those you love. Inarus must die, but the rest can be spared. Choose wisely.

Because if you deny me, I will end him now and move on to your precious Pack."

Wait, what? No, that wasn't the deal.

Fire broke out over my skin, and I crossed my arms over my chest.

"Fuck you. We had a deal. Let him go first, and then I'll go with you."

Worry tore through me. She had a manic gleam in her eyes as if she knew I'd refuse her, and wanted me to.

Of course, I'd refuse. She wanted to kill Inarus regardless of my decision. I couldn't let that happen.

I paced across the rooftop. What could I do? We were separated by over thirty feet of empty air.

I couldn't execute a jump like that, and porting was still beyond me.

I scanned the streets for any sign of Declan and the others. "Come on. What are you waiting for?" I wasn't sure what I wanted them to do exactly, but I needed them to do something. I was trapped on the rooftop, and I didn't like where this was heading.

My mother signaled one of her men to come forward. Dressed in black cargo pants and a fitted black shirt, he had a series of knives strapped to his legs and a rifle slung behind his back.

Human.

There was hope.

I gauged the distance between us again.

"Inarus!" I shouted. "Get up!"

He didn't move.

"Don't do this. If you hurt him, I will never forgive you!" I warned.

My mother shrugged her shoulders. "All parents face the burden of disappointing a child. It's a cross I'll bear for your sake."

Gah! She was insane. What was this supposed to accomplish?

The man walked toward Inarus' prone form. He drew a mace from the belt at his waist.

I sucked in a breath. A mace was meant to deliver powerful blows. It would crush bone and bludgeon an opponent. If he struck Inarus with that, he wouldn't die. Not from just one blow. But it would hurt like hell, and his bones wouldn't just break, they would shatter.

My mother was going to torture Inarus before he died. She would torture and then kill him while I watched.

This was my punishment.

Another man joined the first and lifted Inarus' head before slapping him twice. I saw consciousness bleed into his blue-gray gaze before his eyes met mine.

His head lolled, and he collapsed once more. *What had they done to him that he couldn't hang onto consciousness? Was he drugged?*

The man stood over Inarus and hefted his mace.

I glared daggers at my mother as rage filled my veins. "If you do this, I will end you. It might not be today. It might not be tomorrow. But I will dedicate my life to your demise."

I waited.

She nodded toward the newcomer, and he swung a powerful strike across Inarus' back.

"NO!"

Bone crunched. The sound echoed across the distance, and everything in me screamed to stop it. Inarus made no sound, but his eyes were open now. Whatever drug they'd used on him was wearing off.

He would be awake for his execution.

I pulled at the strands of my dark brown hair and paced furiously. "You can't do this!" I shouted.

Think, Aria. Think.

My mother ignored me.

Viola nodded again, and this time the man struck Inarus behind the knee.

I flinched, and saw the wince cross Inarus' face. I didn't know how much he felt, but when the sedative wore off, he was going to be in a world of hurt.

I headed for the stairwell. I had to stop this.

I tugged on the handle, but the door stayed closed.

Another swing. More bone crunched.

"Stop! Just stop! What do you want? Name your price, and I'll do it, but leave him alone."

She shook her head.

The man swung again, this time on Inarus' right shoulder.

Sonova—

Declan's fury reverberated through the bond. I zeroed in on his location, spotting him on the left as he tried to break through the building's first-floor windows.

Finally.

Two shadows appeared beside him. Derek and Brock.

I just needed to stall a little longer. If they could get to the roof, they could save him.

"Why are you doing this?"

My mother frowned. "I've already explained this to you. You're not a stupid child anymore, Aria. Use that mind of yours, and figure it out."

"No." I shook my head. "I don't mean why are you 'trying to restore order.' I want to know why this?" I waved my hand at Inarus. "Why him?"

"You need to be taught a lesson. This is the best way to do that."

I pulled my fire and formed a ball of white-hot flame in my palm. Before she could take notice, I threw it in her direction.

The fire zoomed straight for her, but missed when she jumped out of its path.

She signaled to the man again, and this time he pulled a knife from his belt and slashed a line across Inarus' cheek. Blood welled to drip down the side of his face.

"Dammit!"

I called my telekinetic power to me. The temple shook. I focused on the knife in my enemy's hand and tore it from his grip.

With a shocked expression on his face, he stared down at his now empty palm as the blade clattered to the ground between our buildings.

"Leave him alone!"

He pulled another blade from his leg sheath. I ripped that one away too.

Then another.

And another.

I could do this all day.

I chanced a glance back toward Declan to find him and the others in a battle with five of my mother's men, each armed with a semi-automatic rifle.

Shit.

"I'd meant for this to go on longer, but you've left me with no choice." She pulled a gun from the back waistband of her pantsuit and aimed it at Inarus. "This will have to do. Remember, you still have a choice to make. Return with me, and I'll spare the others."

The air was sucked out of me in a whoosh. Panic crashed through me, and without thought or effort, only the need to save him, I found myself ported beside Inarus.

Wide-eyed, my mother stood frozen for a beat before she fired.

I threw myself over Inarus, and a blaze of fire speared through my shoulder. I screamed as the bullet tore through muscle and into bone.

The second port brought us beside my vehicle. I panted, and blood dripped down my arm, soaking through the thin cotton of my shirt. I swayed on my knees. Exhaustion pulled at me.

"Declan!" I screamed for him.

Inarus lay in a heap beside me. He didn't move. Blood leaked from the corner of his mouth, and the exposed skin on the back of his neck and forearms was a deep blue-black color. His shoulder was caved in. His leg twisted at an odd angle.

"Declan!" I shouted again.

Gunfire hit the Hummer, and I hunkered down lower, leaning over Inarus to protect him as my vision began to swim.

Declan rushed toward me and slid across the ground as he dodged bullets to reach us. Blood seeped from his upper right chest. "You've been hit," I gasped as he looked me over.

"It's nothing. I'll heal. Where were you hit?"

I pointed to my arm. He gripped the wound, and I winced.

Ripping his shirt off he tore it into strips and wrapped a quick bandage over and across my shoulder and bicep.

"We need to get out of here."

Gunfire continued to hail down all around us. Declan shifted to the back and ripped open the rear door. He hefted Inarus into his arms and shoved him into the backseat. "Get in!"

I climbed in after Inarus as Declan jumped into the driver's seat, and the engine roared to life.

"The others?" I gripped the armrest as Declan barreled down the street.

"They're coming."

I turned to look behind us and saw a fierce lion race behind us followed by a sleek wolf.

"Open the trunk."

Declan pushed a button, and the trunk lifted. I ducked when bullets rang through the space just before Brock and Derek launched themselves into the opening.

Heart in my throat, I crawled over the backseat to reach the rear latch and shut the door.

Another bullet tore into my thigh.

I screamed in pain, but managed to secure the door before slumping back.

"Aria! Aria, are you okay?" Declan's voice sounded far away.

I sucked in a shaky breath.

"Dammit, Aria. Answer me."

My vision blurred, and I turned into Brock's blood coated mane. "Thank you," I whispered. And then it all went black.

Chapter Eighteen

I'd been in and out of consciousness on the way back to the Compound. At some point, Derek had shifted back into his human form and hovered over me.

I tried to ignore his junk dangling between his legs, because he was still very much naked. Despite having been shot twice, I wasn't blind, and seeing Derek naked was freaking me out a little.

I groaned as he ripped through the denim of my jeans to find the bullet wound.

"Talk to me, D."

"Bullet to the left thigh and shoulder. Looks like you already took care of the shoulder, but the thigh one is still in there. I need to get it out."

Declan grunted. "Do it. Have Brock shift to hold her down."

Sweat drenched my body, and a numb tingling sensation took over my fingers and toes.

Brock shifted beside me, and I lifted my uninjured arm to cover my eyes. "Clothes," I groaned.

He chuckled. "Now isn't the time for modesty."

Brock gripped both my arms and pressed me down into the Hummer's floorboards.

"This is going to hurt."

I gritted my teeth, and Derek dug into my thigh. "Ah!" I screamed as his finger probed into the wound. "Stop. Dammit. Stop!"

"I'm almost … there!" He lifted a small silver bullet triumphantly.

I sagged in relief, and everything went black again.

❦

I NEXT WOKE as Inarus and I were rushed into the Compound's med ward.

"What happened?" Dia cried. She stood beside a wide-eyed Robert.

My head swiveled in their direction as I lay on a stretcher. "When did you …"

Robert stood beside me. "We just got back. We got word that her brother was in Sandpoint. She slipped out of the building to make contact, and by then I knew you were planning to retrieve him, so I had her pull out. We just got in an hour ago."

I nodded. "Is he …" my voice trailed off as I searched for Inarus. Pushing myself into a sitting position, I swung my leg over the stretcher. Pain stabbed up from my thigh into my stomach. I gritted my teeth and forced my next words out. "Where is … "

There! I spotted Inarus on the other end of the room. Annabeth and Frankie worked furiously to cut his clothes off of him as Dia paced behind them.

"Please. Oh, God. You have to save him." Dia was crying. Tears streaked her blood-spattered face. She'd wrapped her arms around herself and was rocking back and forth like a child trying to sooth herself.

"Why is she covered in blood?" I asked Robert.

"We had to fight our way out. Scouts tracked her to me, and then ambushed us when we moved to leave."

Inarus made a pain-filled sound. It was like an animal dying, and it left me feeling as though I'd been gutted.

I couldn't tell if what Frankie and Annabeth were doing was helping or only hurting him more.

"He's too far gone." Robert said beside me.

"Fuck you," I growled. "I'm not giving up on him."

This was my fault. I'd sent Inarus to Sanborn Place. I was the reason my mother had turned on him. I never should have let him get involved.

I couldn't lose him. Not now …

"I'm not telling you to give up on him. I'm stating the obvious so you can brace yourself for the inevitable. Psykers don't heal like shifters do. His body can't keep up with his injuries."

I couldn't breathe. Grief and anger choked me. He couldn't die. He just couldn't.

"They're going to take him into surgery. You should lie back down. Declan will be here shortly."

Before I could say anything, I felt the distinct prick of a needle. "Sonova—" my words slurred and my body teetered to the side.

Robert's hands caught me, and he gently laid me back on the makeshift stretcher. "Rest."

And my vision darkened again.

🐾

I AWOKE this time in Declan's room. I lay in his four-poster bed in a clean T-shirt with a fresh pair of yoga pants on.

Someone had cleaned and bandaged my wounds and dressed me.

A blush crept up my neck, and I decided to ignore the fact that someone had seen me naked at my most vulnerable.

I scanned the room, looking for Declan. I needed him, but he wasn't here. His absence left a gaping hole inside of me.

I pushed myself into a sitting position and gently probed the wounds on my thigh and bicep.

I flexed the muscles in my leg and decided they would hold my weight, so I carefully climbed out of bed.

My leg threatened to buckle, but with shaking hands and an iron grip, I hung onto one of the bed posts until my leg stopped shaking.

Taking a deep breath, I took a step.

Then another.

I staggered to one of the leather armchairs and dropped myself into it. Sweat dripped down my back and my limbs shook.

I glanced at the clock. We'd only been gone five hours. Long enough to get attacked, almost die, and crawl our way home with our wounded.

A knock sounded at my door.

I forced myself to sit straight.

"Come in."

Caden walked in, his face sorrowful. "Are you okay?"

"Yeah. Come here." I waved him over, and he took the seat beside me.

"You should be in bed."

I nodded. I was regretting the decision to move. The bed, with my leg elevated, was looking a lot more comfortable right now.

Without saying anything, Caden scooped me into his arms and took me back to the bed. He lay me down, and then climbed in beside me.

We both lay back, and he wrapped his arm around my shoulders.

I could remember lying like this with James when I'd had a shitty day or finished a particularly difficult gig.

"I would have come sooner, but …"

"It's okay. If someone hadn't moved me, I'd have had a hard time leaving the med ward too."

Inarus was still down there. They'd taken him into surgery, and now there was nothing to do but wait.

Inarus had taken a liking to Caden. None of us had expected it, but the two had formed a brotherly bond. Inarus needed a way to redeem himself, and Caden needed someone in his life who wasn't duty-bound to care for him. The two made a good pair.

"Any updates?"

He shook his head. "They think it will be another hour or more."

I sighed. "Then I guess we wait."

Chapter Nineteen

I t'd taken four additional hours of surgery before Frankie and Annabeth emerged. By then Caden had tracked down a wheelchair and wheeled me back to the med ward.

Declan met me shortly after. Annoyance thrummed through the bond, and I chose to ignore it. I knew he wanted me to stay in his room and rest, but Inarus needed me. I needed to be here.

Dia stood in a far-off corner. Her skin was pale, her jet-black hair making her look even paler.

Robert was talking to her, but it didn't look like anything was registering.

She looked catatonic.

Annabeth approached, and I held my breath, dreading the news.

Her appearance seemed to snap Dia out of her fugue-like state, and she rushed toward us.

"Is he okay? Can I see him?" she asked.

Annabeth shook her head. "We've done everything we can," she said. "We don't know if he'll make it. Right now he needs time. We'll monitor him closely for the night, but I'm not optimistic. He sustained massive injuries, and he doesn't heal as fast as we do …"

"But he does heal at an accelerated rate," Dia cut in. "We all do. He's a psyker. That should help, right? He can still pull through."

My eyes filled with unshed tears, and Declan reached down to grasp my hand. I gripped it as hard as I could, and my eyes pleaded with him to do something. There had to be a way for Inarus to pull through.

Declan kissed the top of my head and rubbed small circles along my back with his free hand.

"Only time will tell," Annabeth said. "You can view him through the window, but he's in too critical of condition for anyone to go inside. Over the next few days that might change."

We all nodded and watched her leave the room.

Declan wheeled me closer toward the glass, and Dia came to stand beside me.

We both watched the slow rise and fall of Inarus' chest, barely able to make out his features beneath the wires, tubes, and breathing machine sustaining his life right now.

"He's going to be okay," Dia said.

I didn't know if she was trying to reassure me or herself, but I nodded.

"He will be. He's strong. He'll pull through."

Olivia's message flashed through my mind, but I shoved it away. She might believe a TK had to die. But this one, he had to live.

I didn't think I could handle another death. Not his. Not today.

Inarus had to live.

Aria's story continues in
FORGED BY FIRE
Blood & Magic: Fireboen - Book 6
Grab your copy now on Amazon
Turn the page for a sneak peak—

FORGED BY FIRE

ONE

I f you had trouble of the magic variety, you had two options.

One, you could call the Human and Paranormal Enforcement Division, also known as the HPED. The first problem with this was that in order to call the HPED, you needed to be human. They didn't work for paranormals, no matter how low on the food chain you might be. And if you were human, but the job wasn't entirely human-related, as soon as they got a whiff of supernatural, they were out.

Sure, if someone broke into your house, they were happy to assist. But if that someone was a vampire ex-boyfriend with boundary issues, you were on your own.

The second problem you'd face when calling the HPED was that your issue needed to be small enough that they felt comfortable handling it. The HPED prided themselves in being competent. They would never outright say a job was out of their league.

They would, however, tell you their case log was a mile long, and unfortunately, they wouldn't be able to assist in a timely manner. *Too bad. So sad.*

If you were lucky, they referred you to a mercenary like me. If you were unlucky, they just hung up.

The HPED didn't deal with murder or brutal assaults. They didn't take jobs that actively put their lives in danger.

To be honest, I couldn't blame them. They weren't paid enough to deal with that stuff and unfortunately for them, tax dollars were a thing of the past.

Members of the HPED were paid upon completion of the job. If it looked like an investigation would take several weeks— let alone months— they were going to issue a hard pass when they could find a simple fender bender that they could wrap up in an afternoon.

Option two was calling a mercenary like me in the first place. It's like that children's cartoon saying: "No job's too big. No mercenary's too small." I'm pretty sure it had something to do with pups, but this version worked for me so I rolled with it.

I wasn't the only mercenary in town, but I was one of the best. And I took on *all* the jobs. Didn't matter what the risk was. Didn't matter how long it would take.

And, since I was a nice merc, I didn't charge an arm and a leg if I knew the client couldn't afford it.

There was a time when I would have, but all that changed when a boy was murdered in my city. It was like a switch went off inside of me. Couple that with my boss-slash-surrogate-father being murdered and me inheriting his business, and we'll just say my priorities changed.

It could also have had something to do with being mate-bound to Declan Valkenaar—Alpha to the Pacific Northwest Pack—but I tried not to give him credit when I didn't have to. It would just go to his head.

So with all that said, why the hell was I covered in sweat in an abandoned warehouse when I could have been sitting in my new shiny office, or out in the streets taking down baddies?

I glared at the handsome asshole across the room. His

almond-shaped eyes narrowed further as he smiled and blew me a kiss before giving me the finger.

He was why. *And, I was going to kill him.* I just needed to get close enough to his Asian ass to do it.

Before I could return his lewd gesture, I was forced to jump over the table or risk getting run over by it.

I landed in a crouch as it sailed past me before slamming into the metal wall leaving a dent.

What the hell had I gotten myself into?

Another object—this time a metal folding chair—zipped through the air, aiming for my face.

"Motherfu—"

My feet pounded through the warehouse, each step a loud echo in the near silent room. I sprinted through the wide-open space, zipping past more flying furniture in my haste to get away.

Chair, end table, lamp—they were all out to get me.

Think, Aria. Think. Easier said than done.

You try coming up with a plan when a full warehouse worth of furnishings is trying to kick your ass. I never should have agreed to this. I knew I needed the training. Controlling my pyrokinetic abilities had been a challenge in and of itself. Couple that with my newly acquired telekinetic abilities and I was a virulent ticking time bomb.

But this—this was not training. This was borderline abuse.

Okay, I was probably being dramatic but I couldn't even count the bruises anymore. By the end of today I wouldn't be surprised if I was a giant ball of purple and yellow flesh. I could barely make out my normally sun-kissed, olive skin as it was.

Soft afternoon light filtered in through the dirt-coated windows, lighting the space and illuminating Dia's annoyed frown. *What the hell did she have to be upset about?*

She wasn't the one being pelted. No, she got to stand in relative safety beside Jason as he threw everything he had at me. If it weren't for the spelled cuff still wrapped around her wrist, I'm sure she'd have been joining him in the fun.

"Stop thinking like a mercenary and think like a psyker!" she shouted.

I flipped her the bird.

A smile spread across her face. Oh, when I was through with

—

Chest heaving, I rounded a pillar and ran smack into a coffee table, falling to my knees.

Muscle memory took hold and I jumped to my feet. I kicked the table in the center with my steel-toed boots. It split so I kicked it again, this time breaking it in half.

A smile spread across my face. "Take that!" Stupid table. The karate kid in me jumped for joy.

"You can't win by killing the furniture." Jason Hoang's voice rang through the open space.

I shifted my gaze back to him. He was leaning against a brick pillar with a bored expression on his face. Then again, he was always bored, as though kicking my ass was hardly ever a challenge.

I wanted to punch him. What the hell kind of training exercise was this supposed to be anyway?

An idea formed in my mind, and before I could second guess it, I launched to my feet and sprinted in his direction.

Jason's eyes narrowed. Of Korean and Chinese descent, he had dark brown hair that was shaved on the sides and longer on top. Today he wore ripped jeans and a quarter-sleeve, V-neck white T-shirt.

If I didn't know better, I'd be fooled into believing Jason was the boy next door type with his aloof attitude and easy smile. But he was far from it.

He was the telekinetic mind behind the attacking furniture. Disable him and I'd disable the furniture. Sounded like a solid plan to me.

"What do you think you're doing?"

Oh, wouldn't he like to know.

I smirked and continued my forward charge.

I was five feet away now and closing in when all of a sudden, the air in front of me shimmered, the only hint that he'd formed an invisible wall between us.

I ran headfirst into it and bounced back, falling on my ass.

"Shit!" I spit blood onto the floor and glowered up at him.

"You can't beat every opponent with brute force. You're not a shifter." He flicked his gaze toward Declan, who had so far been a quiet observer. *Asshole.* He was the reason I was here, *training.* You'd think being his mate would keep me warm and sheltered. But no. His idea of keeping me safe was by throwing me to the wolves to get my ass kicked.

I threw my hands in the air. "What do you want from me? I'm trying here."

Dia stomped over and helped me to my feet before giving me a small shove in the shoulder. "You're not trying. You're a telekinetic. Use it."

I shook my head. They didn't know what they were asking. "I fight better with my fire —"

"Too bad. You're never going to take down your mother if you don't figure out how to master both and use them in conjunction with one another. And stop fighting like a street fighter. Look at you." Jason waved a hand in my direction. "You're covered in sweat, breathing heavy, and look like a strong wind could topple you over." He shook his head and then turned to Declan. "Has no one been working with her?"

Declan's emerald green eyes narrowed. "What exactly are you insinuating?" he asked and took a menacing step forward.

That's right, baby! You tell him. I clamped my jaw shut before I could embarrass myself and say those words out loud.

Jason didn't seem cowed. If anything, he was angrier.

"She isn't a shifter, yet her first instinct is to run toward danger and try to beat it into submission. You're handicapping her."

And ensue the rage. It might not look like it based on Declan's expression, but that man was a walking ball of fury.

I ran a hand over my face. I didn't have the energy to try and stop whatever altercation might result from Jason being an idiot.

Up until the past two weeks, Declan had been my trainer. Before him, I'd trained with James—my werewolf best friend who had been conveniently unavailable ever since he went off on some hush hush Pack mission. So yeah, I could kinda see Jason's point, not that I'd ever openly agree with him.

But I didn't have a whole lot of options. Declan and James were two of the only people strong enough to train with me. Sure, both men could tear me in two if they wanted to, but between my pyrokinetic and telekinetic abilities, I could do permanent damage or accidentally kill someone.

I'd been focusing on strength and hand-to-hand training. It was safer. And it was my choice. Declan didn't have the knowledge to hone my psyker abilities. But he was a hell of a fighter. He was doing the best he could with me and it wasn't like I was an easy student.

Declan growled and every hair on my body stood on end. Rather than get involved, I decided to take this opportunity to catch my breath and took a seat on the floor.

It was nice down here.

"Why do you think you're here? Help her or get out. Stop wasting our time."

Jason sighed and turned back to me. "Whatever you learned during your time with the shifters, unlearn it. You need to create new instincts. You need to start reacting with your telekinetic powers first and physical force second. Understand?"

I nodded. Easier said than done, but I was willing to give it a go.

"Okay then. Let's go again."

I heaved out a breath and rose to my feet. That break hadn't lasted long.

This was my fifth training session with Jason and Dia. I was supposed to learn how to better manage my TK abilities. Instead, I tended to get my ass kicked and it was getting old.

I couldn't deny that some of what we worked on did help with my control. The room didn't shake and the floor didn't shudder every time I called on my telekinesis anymore. I wasn't always on the verge of a complete loss of control. And I didn't worry about inadvertently hurting people anymore. But I didn't know how to fight like a TK.

Jason and Dia grew up with their abilities. They called on them instinctually. Telekinesis wasn't natural for me. Fire was. I just didn't understand why they wouldn't let me bury my TK side. If you asked me, being a pyrokinetic was more than enough.

"I can't believe Inarus never went over any of this with you," Dia mumbled as she strode back toward her seat.

I rolled my eyes and decided not to rise to the bait, because in truth, he had. He was the reason I didn't level the Compound when my emotions ran high. He was the reason I could be around the people I cared about. And he was also the reason I knew that, unless I had complete control over them, unleashing my abilities could be catastrophic to those around me.

I knew my telekinesis had the potential to be an asset. I mean, who didn't want more power in a fight? But some mental block inside me didn't want to wield it. Everything in me screamed it was risky. Dangerous.

And no matter how many times I said aloud that I wanted to control it, use it even, in truth, I just wanted my telekinesis to go away.

I eyed the cuff wrapped around Dia's wrist. Her telekinetic abilities were still bound thanks to the spell-worked cuff the Evergreen witches had provided back when she was just one more in an endless line of people who wanted to kill me. It should have come off on its own by now, but it hadn't and I wasn't going to bring it up.

A small part of me wished I had that cuff. But I wasn't willing to sacrifice my pyrokinesis just to have the burden of my TK powers lifted. That cuff was an all or nothing solution. I couldn't pick and choose which powers to smother.

I sighed. Dia might not be the enemy anymore, but she still wasn't a friend.

So I ignored her and rolled my eyes. Inarus had taught me a lot. She didn't know the mess I was before his help. And I wasn't about to lay myself bare before her.

My past wasn't any of her business. And right now, I really didn't want to talk about her brother either. Inarus was the last person I wanted to think about. That way led to nothing but anger and depression.

We still didn't know if he'd survive his injuries.

It'd been over two weeks since my mother—the leader of the Northwest Human Alliance Corporation—had abducted and brutalized him. We'd managed to get him out but not before he'd sustained life-threatening injuries.

He'd undergone surgery, but the damage had been so severe the Pack healers had needed to put him into an induced coma to give him time to heal.

It'd been nearly three weeks now.

Frankie and Annabeth checked on him daily and his vitals were stronger now than before, but we still didn't know when, or if, he'd wake up. Most of his bones had fused back together thanks to advanced psyker healing abilities, but his skin was still mottled with bruises and we didn't know what other internal damage he may have sustained. Gone were the days where we had access to ultrasound machines or x-rays. Now we just prayed and hoped for the best.

It was hard seeing him like that. The stress of it all ate at my nerves. If Inarus didn't pull through, I would never forgive myself.

I shook the thoughts away and focused on my task at hand. He'd wake up. I just had to keep believing that and make sure when he did, I was ready. He deserved retribution and I would give it to him.

The name of the game was to take out Jason. As my self-nominated trainer, he claimed he would whip me into shape and prepare me for the battle we all knew was coming.

The more I worked with him though, the more I thought he was trying to kill me. He didn't pull his punches and I had the bruises to show for it.

A metal folding chair leaped through the air toward me.

"Don't hit it!" Dia shouted. "Use your abilities."

"I know," I ground out.

On instinct, I called my fire to me but quickly realized that the stupid chair would just fly through whatever fire barrier I managed to erect.

Shit. I snuffed out my flames and raised both hands, trying to call on the telekinetic energy buried inside of me.

I didn't use it often. Not with conscious thought. It was volatile and I had no idea how to control it with any sort of precision, so I'd worked at burying it deep inside me. Doing so made it slow to respond but when it did ... I shivered.

The chair closed in and I pulled harder on the ball of energy I knew was buried deep inside of me.

"Come on. Come on." Sweat dripped down my brow. A slow vibration started beneath the surface of my skin, increasing until it created a roar in my ears.

I threw my hands up in front of my face as the chair zipped closer. It slammed into an invisible barrier only inches from my face and hovered there.

I looked up. Relief flooded through me. *I did it. I stopped the chair.*

And then it pulled back, charged forward, and broke through the invisible shield I'd erected around myself, slamming into my face.

Ow!

I fell flat on my back. Blood dripped down my chin and my vision went black before it flickered in and out.

I groaned and rubbed my eyes. When my vision cleared, Dia's face came into view above me. A shit-eating grin spread across her face. "Well, you tried."

I flipped her off and rolled to the side before pushing myself to my feet.

"Again."

"Maybe it's time for a break," Dia suggested.

I waved her off. I didn't need a break.

I leveled my gaze on Jason. "Again."

"Fine by me."

Declan remained quiet but I could feel disapproval radiating from him through our bond.

I shook my head to clear out the dark spots and took a few steps back. I slid my back foot out and assumed a fighters stance.

"Okay. Go."

A table screeched across the floor toward me. I dodged it and blasted it with fire.

"Wrong ability," Dia called.

"I know that!" The table whirled and slammed into my back, knocking me off my feet. I careened forward but managed to stay upright.

"Think faster."

Dia's voice grated on my nerves.

The table came at me again. The sound of scraping metal had me looking over my shoulder to see another table coming in from the rear.

I pulled my TK power to me and melded it with my fire. Air stirred all around me. This wasn't working. At this rate, I was going to be pulverized by furniture. And wouldn't that make for a hilarious headstone.

Here lies Aria Naveed. Pyrokinetic. Mercenary. Idiot killed by a coffee table. May she rest in peace.

I bit my lower lip. I was making too many mistakes. I needed a Plan B.

I stilled and closed my eyes for a moment as I racked my brain. The name of the game was to avoid being hit using only my TK abilities. Which meant I couldn't rely on my fire or my speed.

I snapped my eyes open and my fire surged back inside of me. The two tables closed in.

"Here goes nothing."

Opening the floodgates on my TK abilities, I wrapped both tables in an invisible shield and forced them to halt.

My knees shook. My skin vibrated and sweat dripped down my back between my shoulder blades. It itched, but I ignored it.

Jason shoved against my hold. My teeth clattered and my head pounded. Black spots filled my vision but I held on.

"Not today, buddy. Not today."

I pushed back but it wasn't enough. I was barely hanging on. I could already feel the mental push back. I wasn't going to be able to hold out much longer. Apprehension coursed through me. The blowback was going to hurt like a bitch.

I braced myself in anticipation.

A surge of warmth brushed along my subconscious and I reached for it.

The bond between Declan and I lit up like a neon sign at a strip club. I wrapped invisible hands around it and a cascade of strength surged through my bloodstream.

Adrenaline consumed me and I shoved against Jason with everything I had as I roared a preemptive roar shout of victory.

The tables flew back, each slamming into the opposite wall with an audible thwack.

My knees buckled and I fell to the floor.

I did it. I finally did it.

Declan rushed toward me and pulled me to my feet. I smiled up with a wide grin and kissed him square on the lips.

"Thank you." I was so happy I didn't care that I was acting like a love-drunk idiot.

He scowled, but pulled me close. "Next time, don't wait so long to lean on me."

I laughed. "Hell, if I knew the bond could do that, I'd have taken advantage of it earlier."

Okay, so I might not have. The bond between Declan and I was still a scary thing, but I was happy for it at the moment.

Jason walked over, rubbing his forehead.

"The kickback's a bitch, isn't it?" I snickered and buried my smile against Declan's chest.

He scowled. "I think that's enough for today. Get some rest and we'll do this again soon."

Hopefully not too soon because after today, I needed a nap. Preferably one that lasted several days. And one that maybe included a wine break or two.

Continue Reading...
Grab your copy now on Amazon

Heya!

Thank you for giving Consumed by Fire a read. Did you enjoy Aria's adventure? Are you curious to see what's next in store for her?

Forged by Fire, the final book in the Blood and Magic series is out now! *Just follow the link and Grab your copy.*

—> https://hi.switchy.io/ForgedbyFire

Until next time...

xo Danielle

P.S. Wanna chat? I love hearing from my readers, so if you're interested in staying connected, come visit me in my Facebook group at https://www.facebook.com/groups/danielleannett

Thank You

Thank you again for reading Consumed by Fire and joining Aria on her adventure. I know this book is a bit shorter than previous installments but I promise to make up for it in book 6.

Would you take a moment to leave a review? Word of mouth plays such a big role in a book's success and you can help with just a sentence or two.

Thanks so much!
xoxo Danielle Annett

About the Author

Danielle Annett is a Latinx Author. She's snarky AF, has three rad minions, and likes to write about kick butt heroines in volatile settings. Born and raised in sunny California she now resides in the Pacific Northwest, home to her Pacific Northwest Pack.

Sign up and get notified when Danielle has a new release: https://hi.switchy.io/AnnettNews

Find out more about Danielle here:
Website: www.Danielle-Annett.com
Amazon: https://hi.switchy.io/1AeV
Reader Group: http://www.facebook.com/groups/danielleannett
Facebook: http://www.facebook.com/AuthorDanielleAnnett
Bookbub: https://hi.switchy.io/AnnettBB
Instagram: https://www.instagram.com/authordanielleannett/
Goodreads: https://www.goodreads.com/author/show/7771866.Danielle_Annett
Audible: https://hi.switchy.io/ANNETTAUDIBLE

Stay in Touch

And before you go
Please consider leaving an honest review.
Reviews are like giving your favorite author a hug and we really love *hugs!*

CPSIA information can be obtained
at www.ICGtesting.com
Printed in the USA
LVHW100015290122
709555LV00003B/105

9 781953 264084